P9-CCS-803

The Secret Life of T. K. Dearing

The Secret Life of T.K. Dearing

by Jean Robinson

drawings by Charles Robinson

THE SEABURY PRESS · NEW YORK

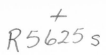

For Don, Lindsey and Carol

1

YOU TAKE most parents. They are worriers. Which is too bad because there is so much going on that you can't let them in on.

For example, clubs, and secret clubhouses way back in the woods where my mother says anything could happen.

She is a gold cup worrier if there ever was one. I am just a normal boy of eleven who is trying to get along the best way I can without telling her everything.

Sometimes this becomes very difficult. Like this past summer when my Grandpa Kindermann came to Primrose Heights and my friends and I—T. K. Dearing*—became involved in a scandal that shook the entire suburb.

I say scandal because I cannot think of a better word.

---

*My full name is actually Theodore Kindermann Dearing, but since Kindermann is a family name and not something you call anyone and Theodore is even worse, I go by T. K. or Teke which satisfies everyone.

But it was not so terrible. We are not troublemakers. I guess we are closer to what you call "involved citizens," at least that's how the *Primrose Heights Leader* described us when they reported the whole mess in the next week's edition.

But I am getting ahead of my story, which began the day my friends and I first suspected something fishy was going on at our clubhouse.

It was a May morning—already so hot and humid you would have guessed it was July—and we were at school. Mr. Talbott, our sixth grade teacher, had just finished reading the scores on the math quiz and it had taken so much out of him that he left for his coffee break.

I waited for a minute, then leaped out of my seat to join the rest of the Buccaneers, who were crowded together in the narrow cloakroom.

I pinned down Dugger, who is really Nelson Douglass Roberts III to everyone but his friends. "Listen, Dugger," I said, "I almost had to eat that note you passed me a minute ago. Don't you have any sense of timing? Mr. Talbott's had his eyes on me the whole morning."

Dugger shrugged. He is not one to be concerned with small details, and since this was an emergency meeting, he could not wait to tell me what it was all about.

"Spies! That's what!" he hissed, waving his pudgy arms

around excitedly and raising his eyebrows so high they disappeared under his bangs. "Someone's been heisting stuff from our clubhouse. Nick and Jerry can prove it!"

Nicolo Gambino, who is Italian-American and maybe the neatest dresser in the whole school, and Jerry Small, the new boy in our development, were the other two members of the Buccaneers. When I asked them if it was true what Dugger had just told me, they nodded vigorously.

"It's no joke, Teke," Nick began, barely able to keep his voice down. "You remember those beat-up bricks that contractor let us take from the old mill site?"

I remembered. They were supposed to be part of the new clubhouse we were going to build when we had all the materials.

"Well, they're all gone! Show him," Nick said, nudging Jerry in the ribs. Squinting behind his glasses, Jerry pointed out the last entry in a spiral notebook. "Fifteen bricks rec'd May 1 by J. Small, Inventory Control Manager. Bricks on hand May 17—none."

"You see?" Dugger exploded, forgetting for a minute that this was a secret meeting and that any one of the twenty-seven other kids in our classroom could be a dangerous spy. "I say we get together this afternoon and check out the place for clues."

Then he remembered where he was and lowered his voice. "Teke, about the flag and the club minutes. We think you should protect them. Nick picked them up last night, and if you don't take them home with you, there's no telling where they'll end up."

I nodded. It was only natural that I guard the club's two most important possessions. I was the only member of the Buccaneers with a room of my own. I was also the president, although the way Dugger took over sometimes you would hardly know it.

Bossiness comes easy for Dugger because he is so insecure. My mother, who is thin as a stick herself, says Dugger is insecure because he is so fat, but that is just something she read in a book.

I could not spend my time worrying about why Dugger was insecure. I had my own problems. Like how was I going to make it to a meeting after school when I had already promised my mother I'd help her?

"Spies or no spies, you guys," I said to them, "we'll have to meet tonight. Today my Grandpa Kindermann's coming for a long visit and what with him being sickly and all, my mother needs help getting him settled."

There was a noise in the hall and Mr. Talbott returned to the room. In a flash we scurried back to our seats. Mr. Talbott sighed, but he did not seem surprised that we were not studying. We were the worst class he'd ever had.

We proved it by scoring even lower on the science quiz than we did on the math test, though Jerry managed to get nearly all the answers right. His father's a project engineer, so I guess Jerry just naturally comes by the smarts in science.

Still, he was as glad as I was when school was out for the day. As usual we both got off clattery old Bus Number 12 and stood in the weeds by the side of the road, waving to Dugger who rode on to the next stop.

Because his mother is an interior decorator who likes to fix up things, Dugger and his family live in an old restored farmhouse that dates back to the Revolutionary War. Jerry and I live down the road in what my father calls a development of cardboard split levels, and Nick lives in town behind his mother's pizza parlor.

It was in the woods just behind our development that we had our clubhouse—a lean-to, really, that we built under the trunk of a fallen tree that lightning had snapped off about five feet from the ground. It was kind of unique as clubhouses go, with the back wall made entirely of flat rocks, the roof and side walls taken care of by the tree trunk, and the front sort of filled in by some old fence boards.

As Jerry and I trudged down Crocus Lane, I wished I was at the clubhouse then, hidden away where no one could get to me, goofing off in the cool shade.

Instead, I was hauling a broomstick-pole flag and the club logbook down the road in the broiling sun, wonder-

ing where I was going to hide them when I got up to my room and wondering even harder how I was going to sneak them up there in the first place.

I did have a room of my own, but my mother wasn't blind. And anything that even looked as if it belonged to a club was going to cause questions. Like: "You aren't going back in those woods again, are you?"

The deepest part of the woods was forbidden to us, mostly because it was too near Potato Tom's place. Potato Tom's an old man—a hermit, actually—who was not exactly the sort of neighbor people in the suburbs expected.

Or felt comfortable with. Especially nervous people like my mother.

I was already keeping so many secrets from my mother that I was practically a nervous wreck myself. Big things, little things, I was a sneak about them all. Take our club flag, for instance. It was one of Mom's best white dish towels, which should give you an idea of how low I would stoop to get what I needed. But how could I tell her I had to have it for a secret club? In Potato Tom's woods?

Believe me, the less my mother knows, the better. I honestly think I contribute to her mental health by keeping the information about me down to the basics and eliminating a lot of unnecessary worry. With me being an only child and all, she worries enough. I mean, if I go bad, *Splat!* it's the end of the ball game. All that fussing at me to brush my teeth and wear my rubbers won't count for a thing.

I do not intend to go bad, but I've never known how to convince my mother of that. So I've always worn my rubbers on muddy days, right down to the edge of the creek where I shuck them off to go wading.

That afternoon, with the logbook and flag in tow, I turned up the driveway to our home, which is a carbon copy of all the other split levels on the street. Inside, I knew the place would be in a turmoil. And all because we were getting ready for Grandpa Kindermann—my mother's number one worry.

2

I SHOULD explain to you about my Grandpa Kindermann. For one thing, he is my mother's father, which makes the whole thing easier to understand.

My mother cried when she came back from visiting him at Aunt Margaret's last January. She did not like to see Grandpa getting old. Most of all, she didn't like to see him getting old at Aunt Margaret's place when she really wanted to take care of him herself.

"Oh, Walter," she snuffled at my father through a handful of Kleenex when we picked her up at the airport that day. "It was a big mistake for Dad to go to Margaret instead of us. I don't care if it was his choice. He looks awful, and no wonder. Margaret just doesn't 'do' for him the way my mother did. Margaret leaves him alone half the time, lets him eat any old thing he can find in the cupboard, and won't even insist that he go to the doctor's for a complete checkup." Then she added that it didn't surprise her. Margaret was lazy even as a child.

"I guess I should be glad she hasn't got him paying room and board. He offered to, you know, but Margaret knows as well as I that he only has the small annuity and his Social Security. Most of what he got for the house went for my mother's medical bills . . . God rest her soul."

My father dug down in his pocket for a fresh handkerchief.

"Walter?"

"Yes, Ruth?"

"If I had Dad here with us, I could look after him. You know, fix him balanced meals, see that he gets out a little . . . maybe even to that nice Soaring Sixties Club they have down at the Community Center."

My father said he didn't think Grandpa was the Soaring Sixties type; what's more, he must like living with Margaret or he would have complained. But my mother replied that that was just nonsense. Grandpa never knew what was good for him; her own mother had told her so.

At any rate, a few days later my mother sent Aunt Margaret a long letter and a pamphlet called *Understanding Your Aging Parents* and five days later the phone rang and there was Aunt Margaret long distance.

I could only hear half of what was said, but I got the impression that my aunt thought my mother was criticizing her and she did not take any too kindly to it, not by a long shot.

It didn't matter, though, because soon after, Aunt Margaret and Uncle Horace decided to go to Europe, and with them gone, it seemed only natural that Grandpa Kindermann come and stay with us while they were away.

The way I figured, it was a lucky break for my mother. She'd have Grandpa right where she wanted him and it would give her a chance to try out some of the new ideas she'd picked up while helping out with the old people Wednesday afternoons at the Primrose Rest Center.

We never guessed she was going to turn the house upside-down getting ready for him. Like she actually re-waxed all the floors with a special nonskid wax and installed a tub rail and a night light in the upstairs bathroom. To me, it seemed like an awful lot of fuss for such a short visit, but then if Grandpa was as bad off as my mother said he was, it was probably necessary.

What worried me most were the new room arrangements and how I was going to keep all our club stuff hidden when Grandpa and I would be sharing quarters for the next six weeks. He couldn't very well share with my parents and we only had the two bedrooms, so what could we do?

Actually, most split levels the size of ours have three bedrooms, but when ours was built, Dad told them to leave out a wall, and as a result my room was twice the size it should have been. But it wasn't crowding two to a room that gave me the jitters, it was the chance that Grandpa just might stumble onto some evidence of the club and give us away.

As I climbed the few steps that led to our front door, I told myself to think positive. After all, what would an old man like Grandpa care about flags and club logbooks? He would be attending the Soaring Sixties' meetings. Or napping. Maybe he stayed in bed half the day.

Once inside the house, I just had time to stash everything in the closet before my mother came down the hall. I didn't need a college degree to guess that she was upset.

"Oh, Teke, I'm so glad you're home. Can you imagine, your grandfather took a cab all the way here from the airport! It was so unnecessary. I was only held up for a few minutes in traffic. Why he didn't wait I'll never know. When I came back home, he was sitting on the doorstep."

To be perfectly honest, this did not seem like such a terrible thing to me, but I didn't say this to my mother. Instead, I threw my books down on the hall table and said, "Well, he's here now. Where? Upstairs?"

My mother nodded. "He's sitting on your bed. Do me a favor, Teke, and see if you can get him to take off his suit coat. He looks so hot. I think he should lie down."

I said okay and started up the stairs. Then, when I was sure she was back in the kitchen, I tiptoed down again to retrieve the flag and the club minutes from the closet. It was too dangerous to leave them there even for a minute. With Grandpa, I could at least take my chances. Pretend they were props or something for a school play.

I was just congratulating myself on this bit of thinking when I heard a loud sigh coming from my bedroom.

"Grandpa?"

"Hello?" It was my grandfather, Ludwig Kindermann, sitting stiff and tall on the edge of my bed.

What my mother said was true. He did seem a lot older than when I'd last seen him six years ago, but his dark gray suit was only a little wrinkled from the heat and his white hair was combed back neatly in a way that almost covered the bald, freckled area on the top of his head.

Right off, he didn't look bad, but then maybe that was only appearances. He was seventy-eight, I told myself. Probably all worn down inside where it really counted.

Quick as I could, I thrust the club stuff behind the door where it would be out of sight. Then I put out my hand. "Grandpa, it's me, Teke!" I said in a loud voice.

"You don't have to shout, boy, I'm not deaf." He looked straight at me. "Your mother send you up here to get me to take off my suit coat?"

He had these X-ray eyes and they were dark as walnuts.

"Well, no sir, not exactly," I hedged, swallowing hard. "But maybe it would be a good idea. It's awfully hot and Mom did say you've been sitting outside on the front step."

"Humph! Just as I thought. 'Take off your suit coat, Dad.' 'Let me get you a glass of water, Dad.' Teke, a man can't even be left in peace to make a few simple decisions for himself."

Once again, he fixed me with this hard stare. "Your mother's a fusser, boy, just like her mother before her."

I was about to agree with at least part of this statement when he gave himself a little push to stand up and crossed the room. "You take your Aunt Margaret. Now *she* lets you be. Though, when you have to live with someone you're never your own boss, you understand, Teke?"

I said I thought so, and he added, "Women, bah. They always want to run things. Fixing up, fussing, *bothering* a man. I tell you, boy, after fifty years of living with your Grandma (God rest her) I've had it. The worm has turned. From now on, I do things *my* way!"

I wondered how this would sit with my mother who likes things *her* way. "Grandpa, I don't know if that'll work. You see, Mom's planning to . . ."

"Meddle in my life? Boy, your mom plans too much, same as most women. That's why it's so cussed hard to live with 'em. You have to go by their rules."

He was right there. 100 per cent right.

"When your grandmother was living, I used to sneak off to the shed. Got some place you sneak off to, boy?" he asked suddenly. "Most boys do."

I shook my head no, but I could feel my face getting hot.

Something told me Grandpa was not as worn-out as he looked. And if that meant what I thought it did, I was going to have to do some pretty fancy figuring just to keep one jump ahead of him.

3

BY SUPPERTIME Grandpa had my mother near crazy. After all, she likes to "do" for people and it really shakes her up when they'd rather "do" for themselves.

Don't get me wrong. There are those who need my mother. Like the patients at the Primrose Rest Center, for instance. Where would they be on Wednesdays without my mother's fussing?

It was just that my grandpa wasn't one of them.

"Boy," he said to me, "I've only been here two hours, and already your mother has me confused with those old people she told Margaret about—the ones she's bothering all the time at the old folks' home."

I learned fast that my grandpa did not consider himself old. That was okay with me. I just thought it was going to be a big shock for my mother.

Downstairs, she was going through all my grandmother's old recipes, planning a meal that would be soft and easy to digest. I was warned beforehand that it would not be chili and garlic bread, but something mildly flavored and well balanced, and just the sort of thing that Grandpa had been accustomed to all his life.

I had this feeling she was going to choose the wrong recipe no matter which one she picked. Grandpa was sick of the old stand-bys. As a matter of fact, he told me he'd already had a hot corned beef sandwich on the plane and a donut and a cup of black coffee at the airport.

I wondered if this was why he looked so uncomfortable. But I was mistaken. Grandpa said he'd accidentally made his belt too tight and that it was pinching him some right in the pit of his stomach.

He still looked a little pinched when we started down the stairs and my father came home. I was relieved because I figured Dad would understand Grandpa's new way of living and be able to pass the word along to my mother.

When he walks in at night with his briefcase, my father looks like he understands everything. He stands tall— about six feet four—and though he's given up his crew cut in favor of longer hair, he still wears white shirts and horn-rimmed glasses. Except for those glasses and the braces on my teeth, we look somewhat alike, though I am a lot skinnier and I almost never understand anything.

There is a good reason for this. I am not real smart. My dad's so smart he sits behind a desk all day and bosses. Then, after dinner, he goes to meetings, and once a week he takes flying lessons. He does all this to stay smart. He is hardly ever home.

So you can understand why it was always bothering him that I was such a goof-off. He wanted me to take an interest in things—the Boy Scouts, the Community Center, anything. I was supposed to be involved so we could sit around some time when he was home and discuss our good causes.

I was not so sure I wanted to get involved in anything just then. What I really wanted was for us to play Monopoly or maybe draw up plans for a bigger clubhouse, one with a real door and plenty of stand-up room.

But could I screw up enough courage to tell him this? No. So I'd just say, "Hi, Dad" when he came in the door and let it go at that.

That night he was all smiles, with a big welcome for Grandpa. "Hello there," he boomed, pumping Grandpa's hand. "Good to have you with us for a while."

"Fancy Dan place you've got here, Walton," Grandpa replied as we headed for the table. "Right out with all the dignitaries."

"It's Walter, Dad," my mother corrected him. "Wal-ter."

My father tried a smile. He may not be home much, but he is still very proud of our house. It cost him a bundle and every year he says they bleed him white just on the taxes.

Naturally, he didn't bring this up at the dinner table. Instead, he answered, "Yes, it's a nice house. Very comfortable."

Grandpa spread his napkin on his lap and studied the living room with a practiced eye. "Not as big as Margaret's place, though," he remarked.

Dad's smile faded. He is a little sensitive about Uncle Horace, his three cars and his sprawling ranch house. Uncle Horace is at least ten years younger than my father and twice as rich. This bugs Dad, because as far as he's concerned, Uncle Horace is still wet behind the ears.

Talk about strained conversations. Before Mom had even passed around Grandma's old-fashioned biscuits, I could

see that Grandpa had a real knack for zeroing in on the wrong subject.

He is not mean. He just has this way of saying what he thinks, and I could see he thought the recipes my mother had chosen were for the birds.

"Not enough seasoning in the meat loaf," he informed Mom as he loaded it with salt and pepper. "Come to think of it, your mother never put enough seasoning in anything either—is this her recipe?"

From the look on her face I knew right away Mom didn't want to hear anything against her mother.

So I said, "Too much spicy stuff'll eat a hole in your stomach, Grandpa. We learned that in science. In a test with mice."

Naturally, this was an out-and-out lie, but it made them wonder.

For dessert we usually had something gooey. But that night Mom served vanilla custard—suggested as a "suitable sweet" in *Understanding Your Aging Parents.*

The phone rang just as my grandfather turned up his nose at the custard. It was Jerry, wanting me to come over and help him with his math. This was a big laugh—he was really calling so I could get out of the house for the club meeting.

My mother was surprised. "But, Teke," she said, "Mrs. Small tells me Jerry is the smartest boy in the class. How could he possibly . . ."

"Be having trouble?" I asked innocently. "It's these bases and exponents. Jerry never had them at the school he went to before."

My grandfather was watching me closely with his X-ray eyes. I couldn't help but feel he knew the whole story was a big lie. In fact his look made me so nervous that I forgot to take the club minutes and the flag to our emergency meeting.

"Well, if you forgot to bring them, where do you have them hidden?" Dugger demanded as I ducked in the door. He was slouched in one corner of the clubhouse by our makeshift stone fireplace, reading the stack of old comic books that we looked at when things got dull.

"They're behind some cardboard cartons on my closet shelf. Look, you guys, I'm not so sure I'll be able to hide much of anything for a while. My grandpa's here—sharing my room—and his eyes are a little sharper than I figured."

"Oh, perfect," Dugger grumbled. "What's that going to do to our plans? Nick scrounged up some tar paper. We were counting on you to take it home."

I glanced up at our crummy pine-branch roof. It looked awful and it didn't keep out much of the rain. Some pieces of tar paper laid across the tree trunk would really help.

"Maybe it'll be safe here just overnight. Then, tomorrow, we can come by and nail it to the roof."

There was a whoop and Jerry burst in from outside, where he had been searching for clues. "Hey, you guys, look! It's some kind of buckle. I just found it outside the door. In the same place we lost the bricks." His ears were getting red and he was looking at us over the top of his glasses the way he always does when he is excited. "What do you think? Do you suppose it belongs to the same person who stole from us?"

Nick leaned forward to examine the buckle. "You know what this looks like? An overshoe buckle. Lots of guys wear this kind. See? Here's the place it tore loose from the rubber."

Dugger gave it a quick once-over and made a face. "That's crazy," he said in his know-it-all voice. "What kid'd wear boots to the woods on a day like yesterday? It wasn't muddy. It's never muddy unless it rains."

He was right. Maybe the buckle had been there for years and wasn't a clue at all.

"I still say we hang onto it," I suggested, wanting to make sure. "Jerry, you keep your eyes out for more clues. In the meantime I'll put this in my room along with the other stuff."

The mention of my room reminded them all that I was now sharing it, but I told them to look on the bright side of things. My grandpa might have sharp eyes, but he wouldn't be here forever. In six short weeks, we could turn my room back into a storehouse.

"Well, almost a storehouse. We'll still have to watch out

for my mother. Tonight, she was just a little suspicious of my excuse to get out."

I did not mention that I thought my grandpa was even more suspicious. It was still on my mind that he knew I was lying. I thought about it all the way home and wondered what he would do if he found out the truth.

When I got home I discovered that I was not the only one with a secret. Mom and Dad had one that was really a whopper.

"Teke, this little visit of your grandfather's is going to be more or less permanent," Mom said. When I looked puzzled, she went on: "What we mean is, your Aunt Margaret's made it very clear that she'd like us to take him for a while. Of course, he doesn't know that yet, which is why it's so important that he be happy here. If he's happy, he'll want to stay and it won't ever be necessary for him to know that Aunt Margaret doesn't want him."

My dad gave me this man-to-man look and a clap on the shoulder. "Don't worry about the room, son. I'll put up a partition and turn it back into two rooms a little later on. In the meantime, just don't say anything to Grandpa, okay? You can keep a *secret,* can't you?"

For the first time in my life, the word depressed me. As I said good night to Grandpa, who was already fast asleep and snoring in the bed next to mine, I decided I had enough secrets. More, really, than I needed. Or wanted.

4

FOR AN old man, Grandpa could have been a power boat on the Schuylkill River. It was my first experience sleeping with someone who snored, and let me tell you, it was something else. All would be quiet, then "Aaghnn-nn!" And the suspense of waiting for the next one was even worse.

But the snoring I could figure out how to stop later. Right then my mind was boggled with bigger problems. Like who or what stole all the tar paper we left overnight in the clubhouse.

It was gone the next day without a trace. A week later, we were still puzzling over the mystery with nothing but a boot buckle to go on.

I had my own private worry about that boot buckle, as I walked home one afternoon from the bus stop. Suppose it didn't belong to a kid at all, but to Potato Tom? And suppose, in his own special way, he was telling us to get out of his woods—by stealing our supplies.

We'd seen Potato Tom, from a distance, a couple of times, and the possibility of having a hermit like him after us did things to my nervous system. I mean, nobody knew much about Potato Tom, just that he kept to himself and wasn't quite right in the head. Some said he got that way after being kicked by a horse a long time ago when he was caretaker on one of the big estates. Now he did odd jobs here and there and sold the few potatoes he raised to the folks he worked for.

He was just a hermit. And it bothered people.

Like once someone wrote to the paper and called his place a rubbish heap, saying it left people with a bad impression of our town, being in plain sight of the commuter train and all.

I did not know about that. I just knew that kids teased him a lot whenever they got the chance, and I, myself, had been scared of him for as long as I could remember.

There was this one time in particular last winter when Dugger, Nick, and I were on our way over to Dugger's place for supper. It was near dark, but still fairly easy to see with the snow on the ground, and we were edgy, having spent the whole afternoon at a vampire movie.

"Let's cut through the woods here," Dugger suggested as we neared his house. "I know it's almost dark, but I want to get home in time to show you this kooky half man–half horse statue my mom threw out in the trash."

Dugger did not want to admit it, but the vampires had scared him.

They had scared me, too, so I went along with the idea in spite of my misgivings. It wasn't that the idea was a bad one, or that Dugger's mother didn't come up with some really unusual trash from her decorating jobs. It was just that the woods after dark was not the best place to get rid of your fears.

"Hey, look at these tracks," Nick said, pointing to some fresh footprints in the snow. "A man dragging something . . . and a dog. Maybe it's a vampire, Dugger, heading for your house."

"Shut up, Nick," I said, eyeing the footprints uneasily. It wasn't the time to be making jokes. At least not about vampires on a night when there was a full moon.

"Dugger? Would your dad be out walking the dog?" I asked. "I thought you told me once that hardly anyone used this path."

Dugger shook his head. "M-my dad's away o-on a b-business trip. And I haven't seen anyone c-come this way for a long t-time."

Nick looked sorry he'd ever said anything. "Well, I was only joking when I said it could be a vampire. Maybe it was just a neighbor dragging firewood. Right, Teke?"

We were holding our breaths when we reached the edge of Dugger's yard. The tracks were there in front of us; for all we knew they led right up to his house.

"Dugger?"

"Shh, I . . . I think I hear something."

He heard something all right. It was the rattle of trash cans, and there in the shadows back of their barn was Potato Tom—and his dog—poking through the rubbish.

He was real, and a whole lot more frightening than the vampires. For one thing, he was wearing a coat so long it just cleared his shoe tops. And on his head he had a fur hat with the flaps down over his ears.

"Hey!" yelled Dugger, without thinking. "What are you doing with my mother's statue?"

Potato Tom wheeled around, his hands still clutching an open gunny sack. It was too dark by then to see his face clearly, but he must have been startled because he gave out this wounded cry. His dog, a scruffy terrier, barked furiously.

Then, before we could call out again, run, or do anything, Potato Tom shuffled off into the darkness dragging his sack full of treasures—the half man–half horse statue among them.

It was a scary experience, partly because we'd never seen Potato Tom that close to our homes before, and partly because he looked so queer.

And he cried out. We'd never heard him make a sound.

After that, I wanted to ask my mother if she knew any more about Potato Tom, like did he get violent or anything, but I didn't dare. She'd have worried, probably even gotten me to confess about the club, and then where would I be? Out of a place to go and three good friends, that's where.

Besides, she had her own problem. Grandpa.

It was as if the grandpa she told me was coming and the grandpa who arrived were two different people.

For one thing, he never took naps.

For another, he never ate baked custards ("Did you ever taste one of your grandmother's custards, boy?") and he refused to wear the new cardigan sweater and soft leather bedroom slippers my mother bought him the first week he was there.

"Only old people wear those leather slippers all the time," he said, taking off his shoes and rubbing a spot just below his ankle. His feet didn't hurt, he reassured me. They just needed a little rubbing.

It didn't matter that the sweater and the loafer-type slippers were just the kind my dad liked.

"Let Walton wear them then," Grandpa grumbled, and wound up wedging the slippers under his rocking chair to keep it from rocking.

"I wish Margaret would cut her trip short and come home," he complained to me. He had had his first taste of the Soaring Sixties Club and he was very depressed. "The place is thick with old widow ladies, most of them husband hunting. You know what they said I looked like? A real spark plug! Spark plug, indeed. I tell you, boy, I'd like to meet the person who came up with the idea for these old-age clubs. They're disgusting. They make a person feel plain . . . segregated!"

Still, he met the rest of them at the Community Center every afternoon, or at least he said he did. Sometimes I wondered. It didn't seem right that he should get so much dirt on his shoes just playing checkers.

But I didn't ask questions. Dirty shoes or not, I guessed Grandpa felt playing checkers was better than doing nothing. And maybe it took his mind off what he really wanted, which was a vegetable garden.

You may think a vegetable garden is a good hobby for an old man. I thought so, and so did my mother until she brought home four tomato plants and a green pepper and found out this was not Grandpa's idea of a vegetable garden at all. He wanted what she called a "little farm" with corn, beans, sweet potatoes, and cucumbers.

"It gets too hot here in the summer to care for that large a plot," Mom told me as Grandpa stalked off to his room. Grandpa would overdo, have a heat stroke, maybe something worse! Then how would we feel?

Terrible, I knew. So I didn't mention the garden again, mainly because my mother was right. The summers around here are too hot for practically everything. Why it was only the last week in May and already Grandpa was feeling the heat.

Four days in a row, when I got home from school, he had

been lying down on his bed after coming back from playing checkers. It was a good thing he was not doing anything more strenuous, I told myself. At seventy-eight, checkers was taking all the strength he had.

This particular afternoon Grandpa insisted he was not worn out at all. "I am just lying here with my eyes closed so I can do some serious thinking," he said to me.

The serious thinking turned out to be about me and why I was always taking off someplace right after dinner.

"Studying again tonight at the . . . ah, library, boy?" he asked, without opening his eyes.

"Uh-huh," I answered uneasily. For a while, I had been using the library as my new excuse to get out. As a story my mother would accept, it worked fine, mainly because the library was a better place for me to be than the pizza parlor, but also because it was only a short distance from our house and I could walk even when it got dark.

Grandpa could not picture me as a boy who wanted to spend every night at the library.

"Must be some big attraction to keep you going there," he said from his bed. "Some pretty girl, maybe?"

"Oh, Grandpa. Who needs girls?"

I tried to look busy, hoping maybe he would lose interest and go to sleep. Keeping the flag and the club logbook hidden from my grandfather had been one of my biggest problems. Without them, he could only guess where I went every night. With them, he had three months of club minutes at his fingertips.

On the top shelf of the closet, way behind some boxes, the flag and the minutes were hidden from view. I was standing on the desk chair, checking to make sure they were still there, when a brown paper bag slipped off the shelf and landed on the floor.

"Hey, what's this?" I said, opening it up. Inside there were six greasy doughnuts—two glazed, two with chocolate icing, and two cinnamon. "Grandpa, these doughnuts! Are they yours?"

His eyes blinked open and he sat up.

"Hello?"

Then he saw the bag and said, "Shh, boy. Keep it down. A few little doughnuts, something to snack on, that's all. Help yourself. Just don't say anything about them to your mother, okay?"

So now I was not only keeping a secret for my parents, I was keeping a secret for my grandpa, as well. It was too much. But we sat down and shared the bag of doughnuts anyway.

"I guess neither of us are supposed to be eating these," I said, biting into the last of the cinnamon doughnuts. "Dr. Bliss, my orthodontist, says my teeth are going to fall out if I keep eating sweets, and you . . . well, aren't greasy things like this hard on your stomach?"

"Nonsense," Grandpa answered, retrieving a speck of chocolate icing that had fallen on the bedspread. "That's just something your mother read in a book. I *like* greasy doughnuts . . . always have. Let your mother give them up if she wants. As far as these go, what she doesn't know won't hurt her."

He gave me the X-ray eye. "Now don't tell me you never keep any secrets from your mother, boy."

I smiled weakly. There was a knot in the pit of my stomach that was either from the last cinnamon doughnut or the sneaking suspicion that Grandpa was on to my phony alibi about the library.

I did not have time to decide which. Downstairs the front door opened and my mother came in.

"Teke? Dad? I'm home, and we have a visitor. Teke, ask your grandpa to come down so I can introduce him to Mrs. Whitfield. She's stopped in especially to meet him."

"Mrs. who?" Grandpa asked, looking a little worried.

"Just a friend of Mom's, Grandpa. She's the president of Mom's women's club and she lives right here in the development."

Grandpa got up, peered out the door and down the hall. "I don't want to meet her," he whispered suddenly. "Tell your mother I'm sleeping."

"Dad? Oh, there you are," my mother said, spotting him in the hall. She moved closer to the stairs. "I want you to meet one of our neighbors—Sally Whitfield."

Mrs. Whitfield's face turned as white as my grandfather's.

"Ruth," she said, breaking the news gently. "I believe we've already met. Your father is . . . ah, our part-time gardener."

5

$\mathbf{W}$HAT a kick. The mud on my grandfather's shoes was not from the Community Center at all, but from Mrs. Whitfield's rose garden.

Mom gasped. "You mean my father . . ."

"Is the man I've been telling you about, dear." Mrs. Whitfield laughed. "He's wonderful! I've been . . . recommending him to all my friends."

My mother grabbed the stair railing for support.

"I . . . I don't know what to say. Dad, how could you do such a thing?"

Grandpa shrugged. "I've got the time. Besides, it's a good way to pick up a little extra money."

The possibility of my grandfather needing money when he was living with us seemed to interest Mrs. Whitfield.

"Sally, it's not like it seems," my mother hurried to explain. "My father doesn't have to work. Dad, tell her you have everything you need!"

Grandpa was silent.

"It's true, Mrs. Whitfield," I butted in. "Grandpa has plenty of money. We don't even make him pay room and board!"

"I should hope not," Mrs. Whitfield said with a sniff, and my mother sighed, "Oh, Teke."

It was a bad time. And it got a whole lot worse after Mrs. Whitfield left and my grandfather was alone with just me and my mother.

"Why did you do it, Dad?" Mom cried, trying to make sense of the whole thing. "No wonder you've looked so tired lately. With this heat, it's a miracle you didn't collapse. Oh, that Sally Whitfield. I'll bet she can hardly wait to phone the whole club."

My mother was as much embarrassed as she was hurt. I mean here she'd been telling everyone how happy and active Grandpa was with his hobbies at the Soaring Sixties Club, and the truth was that he'd only been there once.

But he was going again.

"Oh no, I'm not!" Grandpa snapped, kicking the slippers out from under his rocker. "Either I'm going to hang onto my job, or I'm going to sit here and do nothing till Margaret sends for me!" He rocked hard, all the time keeping his eyes straight ahead, well away from my mother.

"Then you'll have to do nothing, because Mrs. Whitfield certainly isn't going to keep you on anymore. *I won't let her!*"

Backed to the wall, my mother was just as stubborn as my grandfather, which made things very difficult as far as ironing out problems was concerned.

I decided to break the deadlock with a little ironing out of my own.

"Grandpa," I whispered, squatting down by his chair. "At least give the Soaring Sixties another try. Mom told me tonight's meeting is some kind of party! There'll be refreshments!" I paused. "Maybe almost as good as the . . . ah, ones you bring home from Gittleman's Bakery."

You could call it blackmail, but that wouldn't be nice. And it wouldn't be entirely correct either, since I never said I'd tell Mom about the greasy doughnuts. I only hinted at it.

Grandpa gave me this black look. "All right, I'll go," he muttered, "but I won't like it." Then, as he got up and started toward the stairs, he added, for my mother's benefit, "*Margaret* doesn't boss people around till she gets her way. You could take some lessons from her, Ruthie. She's the best daughter [sniff] an old man could have."

It was the first time I could remember that Grandpa had called himself an old man, but I had a feeling it was just for effect. To get sympathy, if you know what I mean— though I couldn't help thinking that, at the moment, my mom needed it more.

She was crying, mostly over Grandpa's comparing her to Aunt Margaret. "How can he think she's so wonderful," Mom sniffled, "when she hasn't even sent him a card? Honestly, Teke, it's getting so I hate to see the mailman come, because there's never anything for your grandfather and he waits around and asks every time."

Fusser that she was, my mother loved Grandpa, and if

she could have gotten away with it, I think she would have sent cards signed "Margaret" herself, just to make him happy.

"Teke," she sighed, "why does your grandfather have to be so stubborn? I'm only trying to 'do' for him the way my mother did. Heaven knows, I don't want him to sit around all day and turn into a vegetable, but I don't want him to overdo, either."

She managed a smile. "Promise me you'll help. Keep your eye on Grandpa as much as you can and try to interest him in something appropriate, like a paint-by-the-numbers kit. They have all kinds of crafts like that at the Community Center and lots of people he can talk to besides."

I promised, but I felt funny doing it. For one thing, I was already keeping Grandpa's secret about the greasy doughnuts and, for another, I wasn't sure what *was* right for him. I mean, I knew how he hated being pushed into things, and yet when he zeroed in on something of his own, it was not always the best thing either.

That night at the dinner table, I tried not to look Grandpa in the eye. It was all right, because he spent the whole time staring at his plate anyway. Just thinking about spending an evening surrounded by those old ladies had thrown him into a depression.

As for myself, I was due at the clubhouse. Overdue. Which meant Jerry had probably gone on without me and

I would have to walk through the woods alone.

Mom was still so upset about Grandpa that she did not give it a thought when I told her after dinner that I had to go to the library again.

"Would you like your dad to drive you?" she asked absent-mindedly as she cleared the table. "He'll be downstairs in a minute to take your grandfather to the Community Center."

"But Grandpa said . . ."

"He wouldn't go? Of course he will. Run up to your room now, Teke, and tell Grandpa Dad's waiting for him."

"M-Mom?" I stammered, nervously. "Grandpa told me he was taking a cab. And it must have come, because he left by the front door about ten minutes ago."

"Oh," she replied, looking very hurt, so I reminded her that Grandpa liked cabs. He took one home from the airport and now here was a chance to ride in one again.

It was a good story, but not a true one. Grandpa wasn't that crazy about cabs. His only reason for taking one was plain stubbornness.

"Don't need Walton to drive me anywhere," he had growled at me just before he left. "If I have to go to that ladies' sewing circle, I'll at least get there myself."

In a way, it was a good thing. There was not much chance of Grandpa turning into a vegetable when he was that hotheaded.

As I started through the woods for our club, I told myself it would all work out fine. Grandpa would learn to enjoy checkers, he would get too busy to bother guessing where I spent my nights, and Mom would never find out about the Buccaneers or the other secrets I kept hidden in my brain.

I forgot all about Potato Tom.

I forgot about him, that is, until I was deep into the woods and got this spooky feeling that someone was following me.

At first, there was only the crack of dead twigs under my feet as I picked my way along the path which was thick on both sides with young trees and wild raspberry bushes.

Then, *Snap!* There was a sound I didn't make just behind me, and when I whirled around, a rustle in the underbrush.

Maybe it's a raccoon, I told myself, but I was not convinced. What reason would a raccoon have for following me? It was my own nerves.

If you think it is silly for a boy of eleven to be nervous, you go into the woods at dusk sometime. It is an eerie place to be. For one thing, the birds have settled down and it is a lot more quiet. For another, it is just dark enough for ordinary things to take on strange shapes.

I took comfort in the fact that I could still hear the cars zooming down Battleson Pike. That and someone's dog barking far off in the distance.

Not that I was stupid enough to think I was so close I

could flag down a car or hail a dog if I needed help. And help I knew I needed as I pushed on, first just a little faster, then with such haste that I was stumbling over every exposed root and jagged stone on the path.

If Potato Tom was following me, he was having as much trouble as I was. It was *Crack! Snap! Rustle!* all the way, although it was getting too dark to see anything when I looked back, and I was too scared to look back most of the time anyway.

My mother had never told me what hermits do when they catch people. For all I knew, Potato Tom was carrying a weapon. I didn't even have our rolled-up flag to beat him off with when he attacked. I had to leave that in my room because my father had insisted on driving me to the library.

Crack! He was still behind me as I left the path and groped my way through the trees toward the club. The ground underfoot was spongy all of a sudden and the vines were thicker, more tangly. They pulled at my ankles and slowed me up, till I was getting sick just thinking about what would happen if I fell. A low hanging branch tore at my hair, and always—in back of me—there were those strange noises.

"Uhhn," I choked with relief as I spotted the light from the clubhouse shining through the trees. It was only a battery-powered camp flashlight, but it was a welcome sight

all the same. I crashed through the brush like a charging bull and took the last few yards up the dirt embankment at a dead run.

"I . . . I think . . . someone's following m-m-me," I sputtered as I flopped down on the dirt floor of the clubhouse and gasped to catch my breath.

There was no use pretending I was in this condition because I was excited about the meeting.

"What do you mean, someone's following you?" Dugger demanded as if I were out of my head.

"Just t-that!" I snapped back between gasps. "Out . . . out there. In the w-w-woods. Be quiet and listen."

Without another word they froze, exchanging smiles all the time to show they thought I was crazy, but keeping their ears open, nevertheless, to make sure.

There was nothing—just the hoot of an owl, a whisper of wind, and far away, the honk of a car horn somewhere on the pike.

Then they were certain I was crazy. So certain, they started to laugh . . . only just then there was a *Thump! Crash! Thump!* and it sounded like a heavy stone rolling down the embankment behind the clubhouse.

"Ohhh," Dugger whimpered, his bravado suddenly gone.

"Maybe it's Potato Tom," Nick croaked and grabbed for the cross around his neck.

Jerry was so scared he couldn't talk, but his ears turned white and he clutched my arm so hard I could feel his fingernails digging through my shirt.

Crunch, Crunch, Crunch. There were footsteps and the funny feeling in my stomach got a lot worse.

I wondered what it would be like to die. And whether they'd put our school pictures on the front page of the *Primrose Heights Leader* when they found our bodies.

Crunch, Crunch, Crunch.

Suddenly, the flashlight picked up the legs and feet of

a man—the rest of him still hidden in shadow—until slowly, and with difficulty, he stooped down and peered inside.

"Hello?"

"Grandpa!" I choked. "What are you doing here?"

All at once, I was so relieved he wasn't Potato Tom that I didn't even realize that we had been discovered.

"So this is the library," he said with a wink.

"Uh-huh," I answered sadly, while Dugger, Nick, and Jerry gave me accusing looks.

6

I T DIDN'T take a superior brain to tell me my friends did not want Grandpa in our clubhouse.

"This was a secret society when we started up," Dugger reminded me, out of Grandpa's earshot. "Just you, me, and Nick. Then"—he gave Jerry a look—"we let Jerry in and now . . . now you're coming around with your family!"

We were standing outside in the dark, trying to figure out what to do about my grandfather and getting nowhere. It was like Dugger to blow his top, but he was way off base making cracks about Jerry. So maybe it had taken a little convincing on my part to get him into the club when he first moved here. Since then, I figured, he'd proved his worth.

I reminded Dugger how disorganized everything was before Jerry's record book. "So don't act like you're sorry there aren't just the three of us. Besides, who said I brought my grandfather here in the first place? I didn't *bring* him anywhere. He followed me!"

"Followed you?"

"That's right, followed me. He needs someplace to go and he can't stand all those old people over at the Community Center."

"What's the matter with them?" Nick asked, intrigued. "They're about the same age as your grandpa, aren't they?"

I nodded. "But they're pretty disgusting . . . and ladies, mostly. My grandpa's had his fill of old ladies. What he wants now is a new way of life. A chance to find his own friends, you know what I mean?"

"I know what you mean," Dugger grumped, "and I'm all for it. Just don't get any ideas about whose friends he's going to find! You're crazy if you think we're going to let him join our club!"

"Yeah," Nick added, "it would be almost as bad as asking our parents. I mean, what kind of secrets can we have with your grandfather around? It's plain stupid."

I waved my arms to cancel out all their protests. "Listen, you guys, I never said anything about him joining. Just let him stay for tonight's meeting. He's supposed to be at the Community Center and if he comes home early, he'll be in trouble with my mother."

The idea of anyone as old as my grandfather getting in trouble with my mother really set them back. But not for long.

Pretty soon Jerry asked, "What about the club? Will he tell on us?"

"I don't think so," I said, a little uncertain myself. "Like

I said, Grandpa's real understanding. He has this thing for secret hideouts. He knows from experience how important it is to sneak away."

"Ha!" Dugger snorted. "My grandfather doesn't understand anything. He just pokes his cane at people and says, 'Look here, young fellow, in my day . . .' What makes your grandfather any different?"

My grandpa wasn't Nelson Douglass Roberts I, president of the Roberts Box Company. He was just Ludwig Theodore Kindermann, the Nobody, who used to sneak out to the shed to get away from my grandmother and who knew all about needing a place to go when things got bad.

". . . So, come on, you guys, please? He won't bother anyone, I promise. Just give him a break. Remember, you'll be old yourself some day."

I threw in this last because it's something my mother was always saying—usually as she went out the door to the Primrose Rest Center when I was wishing she'd stay home and bake cookies.

"Okay, okay," they agreed finally, "but just for tonight."

"And only if he promises not to tell anyone," Jerry reminded me.

We ducked back inside where Grandpa was patiently waiting.

"Everything all settled?" he asked pleasantly.

"All settled," I said, brushing some dirt off the top of a small vegetable crate before handing it to my grandfather.

"Here, Grandpa, sit on this. Then we'll go on with our meeting. We don't have much time."

I gave him the crate so he would not have to sit on the dirt floor. There was no sense letting him get a chill, I reasoned, remembering all the warnings my mother had given me about the damp ground. My friends and I were comfortable enough on Dugger's old camp blanket, but that was because we were just kids. Kids don't catch colds sitting on the ground; parents do. And Grandpa was twice as old as most parents and achy already; with a combination like that he had to be twice as careful.

The meeting came to order.

"Will everyone please pipe down?" I shouted, banging our cutoff croquet mallet on a wood box. "First, we'll give the secret sign and the secret word. Then, we'll hear Jerry's report on the latest inventory."

I was just following our usual routine, but right away we were in trouble. With Grandpa there, no one wanted to give the secret sign and the secret word.

I waited. Then, finally, after a long silence, Jerry whispered, "Skoal," and made the sign of the crossed swords. He figured like I did—it was too late for secrets. If Grandpa knew about the clubhouse, there was not much point keeping the password from him.

"Skoal," I replied, getting Nick and Dugger to follow suit.

"Skoal," Grandpa repeated happily.

From the long faces, I could see the guys did not like

Grandpa giving the secret word. They liked it even less when he held up the secret sign.

"Hey!" Dugger whispered in protest. "You said he was just a guest. He acts like he is already a member!"

I ignored this and hurried on to the next order of business. "Jerry, what's your report? Any more . . . ah, developments in the current inventory crisis?"

Jerry took my clue to play it cool. "Nothing new," he hesitated, looking out of the corner of his eye at my grandfather. "Just . . . uh, the usual problems we've encountered all along. We . . . we need more nails. The can of them we had sitting on the shelf over the fireplace is . . . uh, used up."

"I'll pick up some nails for you tomorrow at the hardware store," Grandpa offered. "Just let me know what kind and I'll bring them to the next meeting."

He was very enthusiastic. Too enthusiastic, if I correctly interpreted the looks I was getting from my friends.

"Your grandfather thinks he's coming to the next meeting," Dugger hissed at me as we shut up shop and headed for home. Jerry and Grandpa were waiting outside. Nick was at the door, swinging the camp lantern.

"Now don't get all uptight about this," I told them, keeping my voice low. But it did no good. Dugger and Nick were definitely bugged. Even Jerry gave me the cold shoulder on the way home. The only one who was the least bit talkative was my Grandpa Kindermann.

For him, the evening had been a complete success.

7

THE NEXT day at school, not a single one of the guys would speak to me. When I finally did corner them in the cloakroom, Nick broke down and said, "Look, Teke, maybe the club wasn't . . . ah, such a good idea."

"Yeah, we think we should disband it," Dugger added.

"Leave the clubhouse for whoever's been stealing from it and forget the whole thing," Jerry put in.

Talk about loyalty. Boy! Even Jerry was against me. And all because of what? Something that wasn't even my fault.

"Hey! I thought we Buccaneers were supposed to stick together. You guys aren't even giving me a chance. I'll talk to my grandpa. Honest. I'll get him to promise he won't ever set foot in our clubhouse again."

"Nice trick if you can do it," Dugger muttered and the others nodded.

We called a truce and I wondered how I could break the bad news to my grandfather. He wasn't likely to find another club that would let him in. And, at his age, he was probably too old to start one on his own.

Actually, I was kind of irritated. I mean, here I was, minding my own business and trying to enjoy a normal boyhood and what did I get? A grandfather who wanted to enjoy it with me.

Because of him I had almost lost three friends. Not to mention a clubhouse—the best one we'd ever built and the only one of its kind in maybe the whole area.

It was unfair. Oh, maybe there was no rule saying an old man couldn't be in a boys' club, but then it wasn't something you saw every day either.

I was determined to set the matter straight once and for all. A few words, properly respectful, of course, would do the trick. Except I didn't know the words and there was no one around to tell me.

It didn't help that Grandpa was in another depression when I came home from school that afternoon. He'd been down in the basement trying to soak his aching feet when my mother discovered him and had a fit.

"His feet hurt him, Teke, but he won't let me buy him comfortable shoes. 'These are plenty good,' he says. Wouldn't you think he'd realize feet can change? That he might need a different style?"

"I don't think he wants to admit he's changed at all."

"If I could just get him in to a doctor," my mother sighed. "Here, Teke, take this vitamin pill up to your grandpa and see if *you* can get him to swallow it. I put one out for him every day, but he won't take them. Says they're the same brand your grandmother used and if they didn't help her they aren't about to help him either."

My mother figured that if he wouldn't go into the doctor's for a checkup, the least he could do was take vitamins. And yet, when I started upstairs with the pill, I wished she'd just lay off for a while. Grandpa was no kid. What could it matter if he skipped his vitamin on a day when he was feeling moody?

Still, it was not my job to reason why. Only to keep everyone's secrets and make Grandpa so happy he would not care when he found out he was stuck with us for good.

It had turned me into a worse liar than I was before.

"Grandpa," I heard myself saying, "Mom's going to have my head if you don't take this vitamin. I know you don't need it—anyone looking at you could tell you don't need it—but you know Mom. Take it, please, just to humor her?"

"I don't know why I have to be spied on all the time," he grumbled. "Your mother thinks my feet hurt and the truth is I was just softening my toenails. Got to trim 'em, you know. Can't get holes in my socks."

He picked up the pill and turned it over in his hand. "A waste of money," he observed and swallowed it with half a glass of water. "Skoal! Teke, what have we got on the agenda for this afternoon?"

"Grandpa, about the club . . ." I began, but it did no good.

He was ready to go. He even produced a small sack of nails he had purchased just that afternoon at the hardware store.

But, Grandpa, the boys and I . . . well, we don't think you should . . ."

"Spend my own money on a few nails? Nonsense, boy, I'm glad to do it. Just being able to sneak away to a place where there are no meddlesome old ladies is reward enough for me."

I tried again. "Grandpa, you don't understand. It's . . . the meetings. I don't want to disappoint you, but the club rules say that . . ."

"Old men can't come?" Grandpa asked after a long silence. He looked so heartbroken I couldn't bear to tell him this was the truth.

"No, Grandpa, it's just that you have to be a member before you can . . . uh, give the club sign and the secret password."

He was relieved. "Oh. Well, that's okay. If it helps, I'll pretend I don't even notice when we come to that part of the meeting."

Somewhere, from way back in my mind, a small voice said to me, "Teke, you have not kept your promise." The small voice did not lie. I had done worse than that. I had practically given Grandpa the go-ahead to attend all the meetings he wanted.

It was going to be a bad time for me when the other guys found out.

"All alone?" Dugger asked me suspiciously as I ducked in the clubhouse about seven that night.

"All alone," I answered, giving him the sign of the crossed swords. I did not tell him that Grandpa would be along later. It was enough that I was just back in the Buccaneers. The knottier problems I would deal with as they came up.

"Teke, we were just talking about setting a trap," Nick said, looking up from a stack of well-scribbled papers. "You know, something that will really stop whoever's stealing our stuff."

"I'm for stones," Jerry burst out enthusiastically. "A pile of them balanced on the roof over the door. One finger on the string stretched across the entrance and *Powie!*" He flailed his arms in every direction. "Boulder Dam crashing down on the spy's skull."

Dugger shook his head. "You nitwit. That could kill someone. Suppose it's a little kid. Did you ever think about that? A pile of stones could pulverize him . . . smash him right down into the ground!"

It was a grisly picture. So grisly that, for a moment, no one said anything. Then Nick suggested, "How about snakes? Lots of people are scared of snakes. We could leave a couple of snakeskins lying around outside, maybe even let Jerry's pet snake Sidney loose in the clubhouse. How about it? Our thief would think the place is crawling with snakes! Probably stay away for good."

Dugger shuddered. I was the only one who knew that he was not big on snakes, skinned or otherwise. If we took Nick's suggestion, we would lose more than a spy. We would lose our vice-president and then where would we be?

"I have a better idea," I told them, thinking fast. "How about a sign *warning* people about snakes? Something in big letters that we could put right on the pile of wood outside where the snakes would most likely be."

Dugger looked relieved. "Yeah, that's not bad. What do you think, you guys? It won't kill anyone, and it might scare away whoever's stealing our supplies, especially if it's some little kid."

They were like me. They did not want to discuss the possibility that the spy might be Potato Tom. Still, the possibility was there, and we all knew it when Nick mulled over my idea and said, "Okay, I vote we try it. I just hope we're right guessing this is the work of a kid. It might not be a kid at all," he added, his face solemn.

"Yeah," the three of us agreed reluctantly.

We were startled out of the grim silence we had fallen into by the rustle of a bush just outside.

"Hello?" A cheery voice called.

"It's your *grandpa!*" Jerry groaned.

"Teke, you promised! Didn't you tell him he couldn't come to any more meetings?" Dugger stormed. "You said you'd take care of it . . . this afternoon!"

I shook my head. "I just . . . couldn't. I'm sorry, you guys. If you want, I'll resign or something. Maybe that's the only way."

Grandpa peeked through the door with a puzzled smile. "What's . . . [puff] the only way, Teke?" he asked, obviously short of breath. "Sorry I'm late. Had a stop to make and [puff] it took me a lot longer to walk through the woods [puff] than I figured."

While I was studying his face, trying to decide if he was all right, I caught a whiff of something good. It was a sausage pizza, which Grandpa slid out of a flat paper sack. With it, he'd brought along five cans of cold soda, four of them tucked in the pockets of his old suit jacket.

"Hey, neat!" Jerry said, eyeing the hot pizza like a person who had been without food for six weeks.

"Yeah, pepperoni pizza, my favorite!" Dugger exclaimed.

There is nothing like food to patch up a misunderstanding between friends. By the time we had polished off the last crumb of Grandpa's generosity, the boys were looking at him in a new light.

"There's no reason why I couldn't screen in a front door for you," Grandpa suggested, slapping at a moth. He was breathing normally again. "A few cents for screen and a little time, that's all it needs. Also, could you use a storage box?" he asked as he drained the last of his cream soda.

"Seems like every club should have a padlocked storage box. I could put one of those together, too."

In twenty minutes, he'd made himself so valuable that Dugger called a conference outside.

"Teke, maybe we were . . . uh, in too much of a hurry when we said your grandfather couldn't join our club. He doesn't act like most old people. Maybe he could be . . . an honorary member."

"Yeah," Nick seconded the motion. "Honorary, with

special permission to attend all the meetings he wants."

Jerry was still licking the cheese and tomato sauce from his fingers. "All in favor?"

The motion was carried, which just goes to show you how quick things can change. One minute I was out of the Buccaneers with no friends at all, and the next I was the grandson of the most popular Buccaneer of them all.

There was only one thing that worried me. To be even an *honorary* member, Grandpa still had to sign his name in blood for the blood oath.

"Do you think you should?" I asked, remembering my promise to watch out for him. I mean, here he was, barely recovered from his trek through the woods. Was it right that we should weaken him still further by taking blood from his finger?

The guys sensed my concern.

"We could fake it, Mr. Kindermann," Nick said, obligingly.

"Yeah, use red ink or something just as good," Jerry added.

"No, take my blood. A blood oath is a blood oath." To our dismay, Grandpa stretched out his hand, true blue and every inch a Buccaneer to the very end.

Dugger got the shakes.

"H-h-here, Teke, you d-do it," he said, handing me the pin with a shudder. There was a reason he was giving up his official duty of pin sticking. If anyone in the Club was going to be responsible for my grandfather's winding up dead, it was going to be me.

Nick lit a match. "Wait, Teke. You . . . you'd better sterilize it first. You don't want to take any chances."

He held the flame under the pin for a long time, and after it went out, I let it cool for a lot longer. Then, because there wasn't anything else I could do, I touched the pin —ever so gently—to my grandfather's finger.

He winced, but did not cry out.

Murderer, I told myself, and for a long second we stared at the spot where the pin went in. Then, suddenly, it welled up red. A bright, healthy red, the same color as my blood when I had my last checkup.

Somehow, I had expected it to be a sickly orange, or maybe even the color of canned salmon. But then, Grandpa had been full of surprises. Having good blood was just one of them.

". . . Ever faithful," he repeated, "and true to the cause of the Buccaneers. So be it."

"Skoal."

"Skoal!"

That night Grandpa slept peacefully despite the pizza. I lay awake for a long time. His snoring was getting worse. I wondered if it was just from all the activity or whether cream soda had some effect on his breathing mechanism.

8

It was killing my mother that she could not get Grandpa in to the doctor for a checkup. Nothing, not even her special menus and the daily vitamin seemed to give him any pep. He looked tired. A little more so every day.

Grandpa claimed he'd never felt better in his life and that if he wanted to sleep a little later in the morning, it was not because he was worn out. It was because my father used up all the hot water shaving and it was at least another hour before there was enough for anyone else.

I knew different. My grandfather was putting all the energy he had into the Buccaneers. When he joined, I figured he would just come to meetings. Soon, I learned he was hanging out at the clubhouse a good part of each day —sawing and hammering, putting up a screen door, and generally tidying up the area around the creek so we would have a place to fish.

I told him, "Grandpa, relax a little. Leave the hard stuff for us. Now that school's out, there's a whole summer ahead of us. The guys and I have weeks and weeks to get all this done."

He wouldn't listen. Instead, he just smiled and went back to work. "Teke," he said, "you'd better watch it. If you aren't careful, you'll wind up being a bigger fusser than your mother."

So there I was. Afraid that I'd let Grandpa take on more than he could handle, but too chicken to blow the whistle on him and have him mad at me forever.

I didn't have the heart to spoil Grandpa's fun. Not when it was just beginning to put a smile on his face and take his mind off the whereabouts of Aunt Margaret. She'd finally sent all of us a card from Paris, but nowhere on it did she mention anything about Grandpa. It was all we could do to make excuses for her, saying that postcards were too small for big messages and that surely Aunt Margaret would send him a long, personal letter when she got home.

If you ask me, grownups shouldn't try to keep secrets, they are so lousy at it. My parents' plan wasn't working; it wasn't going to work. Grandpa wanted to go back to Aunt Margaret's and he wanted to go back soon. All the extra attention my mother had given him had only affected him the wrong way.

That was why I kept my mouth shut about Grandpa's membership in the Buccaneers, no matter how worried I was about him. It was the only good thing he'd have to fall back on when my parents finally did tell him the truth. He certainly hadn't changed his mind about the Soaring Sixties and he wasn't likely to start painting-by-the-numbers for my mother, not when she'd been a party to the whole rotten scheme.

Actually, I wasn't sure Dugger and the guys would let Grandpa quit the Buccaneers even if he wanted to. He was First Honorary Building and Planning Chairman. He was also the only one of us who had the money to bring in pizzas, canned soda, doughnuts, potato chips, and cookies.

Talk about good friends. They weren't even real upset when he spoiled our snake trap. After all, Grandpa had no way of knowing that the sign was there to scare off a thief. He thought we'd put it on the woodpile because *we* were afraid of snakes ourselves. So he took down the sign and re-stacked the wood just to show us we were safe.

We could have told Grandpa about our missing supplies, but it wouldn't have been smart. Just watching him so that he did not work too hard was difficult enough. If he was out of our sight, trailing spies, almost anything could happen.

What this "anything" might be I didn't know, but I thought it would be a good idea to look into it, just in case. Without a real doctor's opinion, though, I was forced to do some research on my own. It was not too complete. As a matter of fact, all the information I could gather was from the current issues of *Everyone's Health* in my orthodontist's waiting room.

Dr. Bliss knows from nothing about old people. At least he had very little to say when I asked a few questions. What he was mainly interested in was my braces and how they were getting so gunked up with food when I brushed my teeth after every meal and never touched candy or other snacks between times.

So *Everyone's Health* was the only authority I could turn to. And all the June and July issues had to say about old people was that they should drink plenty of liquids, especially in the summer when it was hot.

Much to my surprise, it did have an article on snoring and what persons who don't snore could do about those who do. Poking the snorer in the ribs was one cure. Tying a knot in the back of their pajama string so they would sleep on their stomach was another.

I could not bring myself to put a lumpy knot in my grandpa's pajamas. So I just jiggled him from time to time on his shoulder and lay awake the nights it didn't seem to work.

"Grandpa," I said to him one afternoon just after I'd come home from the clubhouse, "have you ever tried sleeping on your stomach? Last night . . . well, last night you were snoring again, and I read someplace that sleeping on your back is what causes it."

Grandpa was very apologetic. "I will try, Teke. And if I

start in and you see me on my back, just jump out of bed and roll me over."

He was sitting in his chair rubbing the sore spot on his foot.

"You weren't at the club this afternoon, Grandpa," I said, looking the other way. "Did you take a nap? Nick and Jerry caught this big frog. They wanted to show it to you before they let it go."

"Couldn't make it," Grandpa answered mysteriously. "I had other business. Matter of fact, I won't even be there tonight. Your mother and dad are having company and they want me to stick around and join in for a little visit."

I found this peculiar until Mom told me who the company was—Dr. Hollisey, the youngest member of the Primrose Heights Medical Center and our new family doctor.

"Now, don't tell your grandfather who he is," my mother warned. "It's the only way I have for a doctor to look at him! A complete checkup seems out of the question, but if Dr. Hollisey could just see him, maybe even win over his confidence, well..."

"Mom, I wish you wouldn't try to keep any more secrets from Grandpa. Things are bad enough already."

I was referring to the letter he had finally received from Aunt Margaret. It was a nice enough letter, but it skirted around without saying anything definite, such as the date Grandpa was to return to Aunt Margaret's. I suppose that, like my mother, Aunt Margaret was still hoping Grandpa would learn to love it with us. But Grandpa had not, and the tone of the letter had put a worried look on his face that I did not like.

". . . Please," my mother begged me, "just go along with things when I introduce the doctor as Jeff Hollisey. What harm can come from it? Maybe he will be able to give us some advice just seeing your grandfather up close."

It was possible. For myself, I knew that even a few words would be better than *Everyone's Health*. The doctors who wrote for it had never even met Grandpa.

I was at the clubhouse when Dr. Hollisey arrived, but when I got home an hour or so afterwards, things were very cozy. My dad was serving drinks while my mother was urging my Grandpa to tell the doctor about the Soaring Sixties Club.

"Oh, Teke," she called, beckoning me in. "Say hello to . . . ah, mmph Hollisey."

"Hello, sir," I replied politely. Then, because I felt as guilty as anything, I added, "Skoal, Grandpa, how're you doing?"

My mother beamed. "Teke and his grandfather have such a nice relationship," she told the doctor. "Private words and signs. Why, they're like a couple of best friends the way they're always whispering around here."

I was not so sure Grandpa still figured me for his best friend a little later when the hospital called for Dr. Hollisey and the whole scheme went down the tubes.

"Hello?" My father said into the kitchen phone in a voice loud enough for all of us to hear. "Who did you say it was? I'm sorry, you'll have to repeat that. We seem to have a bad connection."

Things grew quiet where we were sitting and Dr. Hollisey looked at my mother with real concern.

"Could it be my answering service? I told them where I'd be."

There was a momentary silence in the kitchen, then my father said, "Oh, yes. He's here. Just a minute and I'll call him to the phone."

Dr. Hollisey stood up, all crisp and professional. "Is it the hospital?" he asked as my Dad stepped round the corner with the receiver in his hand.

"The one down in Prospect Hill. Sorry I didn't catch what they said for a minute, Doctor. There's quite a lot of static on the line."

What with the static and the unexpectedness of an emergency call, both of them forgot about my grandfather.

A stupid play.

Grandpa pulled himself to his feet and stood tall. "So your friend's a doctor, is he? What did you want him to do? Look me over at ten paces and report back to you on the sly?"

Before my mother had a chance to reply, he stomped upstairs, leaving me to trail behind—miserable because I'd betrayed a fellow Buccaneer.

"Grandpa, I'm sorry. I never should have agreed to go along with it."

"That's okay, Teke. You were just doing what you were told. Boy, have you seen my ruled tablet? I'm going to sit down and write Margaret that I want to come home. *She'd* never pull a stunt like this. Why, when she hears what I've had to put up with for the past two months, she'll send for me right away!"

9

I TRIED to talk Grandpa out of mailing the letter, but it was no use.

"Shouldn't have come in the first place. Should have told Margaret I'd stay alone while she was on her trip. No reason I couldn't have done that. No reason at all."

"But Grandpa . . ."

"Oh, I don't mean to say I've regretted any of the time I've spent with you, Teke . . . or the rest of the Buccaneers. I'm going to miss you. If it weren't for you, I'd have written Margaret weeks ago."

Difficult as it was going to be for him to give up his membership in the Buccaneers, he was determined to leave our house as quickly as possible. "Tomorrow wouldn't be too soon, boy. All Margaret has to do is tell me which plane!"

I knew what Aunt Margaret was going to tell him, and it wasn't going to be which plane. Like my mother, I'd hoped Grandpa would be so happy with us he wouldn't want to go. Then it would be *Grandpa* telling Aunt Margaret he wasn't coming back instead of the other way around.

It was going to be a sad day when her reply arrived and the truth was out. The very thought of it was so depressing that I was hard put to keep my mind on my other problems.

Like the clubhouse thief.

"Teke, you're not listening!" Dugger said, giving me a poke in the ribs. "We've fooled around long enough. All of us know the spy isn't some little kid. It's Potato Tom and the sooner we face up to it the better."

The four of us were in the woods, picking our way back to the clubhouse after a top secret meeting at Mrs. Gambino's pizza parlor. It was muddy, from a hard rain the day before, and that morning we'd discovered several large footprints just outside the clubhouse door.

They did not belong to some little kid.

They didn't even belong to my grandfather, because they were not his size and he had been home—holed up in our room—when they were made.

"Teke, you're the greatest," Nick said admiringly. "How'd you manage to sneak away with one of your grandpa's shoes so we could check his size?"

I shrugged. "He slept late. Besides, when he's in our room with the door shut, he keeps his shoes off most of the time anyway. His feet hurt. It's just one of those things that comes with getting old."

I played it modest, but still I kind of enjoyed Nick's praise. After all, it had taken a lot of running around—returning the shoe to the house before Grandpa woke up, and then catching up with the guys at Mrs. Gambino's.

When we got back to the clubhouse, Dugger studied the footprints again. "You know, I don't think these were made with shoes at all," he said. "They're more like boots, overshoes maybe. Overshoes with . . ."

"Metal buckles?" I asked, suddenly putting two and two together.

So the first clue we found was a clue after all! "Good thing we saved it," Jerry said, his voice cracking a little. "Sometime when we see Potato Tom in overshoes, we can check to see if he's missing a buckle."

"I say we sneak up on him now," Nick suggested stoutly.

"Yeah," Dugger agreed. "H-hunt Potato Tom down on his own g-grounds. Find out for sure if he's been stealing our stuff."

"Can't we just call him up and ask?" Jerry whispered with a nervous laugh. He was trying to be funny. None of us liked the idea of tracking down a real hermit. It could be dangerous. It could be the most dangerous thing any of us had done in our entire lives.

"Remember," Dugger said in a low voice, "if any of us are c-caught, he will disavow knowledge of the other three.

Got that?"

"Got it," we replied.

The zero hour was upon us, but no one moved. "Come on, you guys," I said finally. "Let's get this over with. Tomorrow my grandpa will be around again and you know we can't take him. He'd get too tired, maybe even slip on the mud or something if we had to run."

It's a good thing he had other business to attend to, I told myself. Keeping *me* out of the clutches of Potato Tom would be difficult enough. If I had to worry about Grandpa too, I would be a nervous wreck.

I was practically a nervous wreck anyway. To be perfectly honest, hermits frightened me, even in broad daylight when hardly anything was scary.

"With a little bit of luck," I muttered under my breath, "Potato Tom could put us away for good, then starve us till we're nothing but skin and bones and feed us to the rats when it's all over."

"Ughh, Teke! If you have to think of those things, keep them to yourself, will you?"

It was Dugger. He was just in back of me on the path, clomping down like a baby elephant on every last twig, pine cone, and pebble that would make a noise.

"Be quiet, huh, Dugger?"

He stumbled over a root.

"Sorry."

We were in dangerous territory. Deeper in the woods than we had ever been—so deep we could see Potato Tom's shack just ahead in a small clearing.

I should tell you something about his place; it was at the wood's end. Beyond that, there was just gravel and the commuter train railroad track. Potato Tom's shack and the acre or so of land surrounding it were kind of stuck in between.

Up close, you could certainly see that the shack was run-down. The rough wood siding was gray, like it had not been painted in years, the roof was patched with an odd assortment of shingles and the outhouse door was falling off its hinges.

"Boy, did you ever see such a mess?" Dugger whispered distastefully. "Look at all that junk sitting out in the yard. He must haul it home from the dump. No one could accumulate all that by himself."

We were about fifty feet from the back porch. Alongside it, in the tall weeds, were a rusty old wringer washer, some tires, and a bashed-in garbage can. Past that there was a garden, or what looked like the remains of a garden, newly washed out by the last rain.

Maybe the only thing pretty about the whole place was a huge magnolia tree. It stood alone in the hard-packed dirt, shading the entire shack, its gnarled branches thick with glossy green leaves.

"Hey look out!" Nick warned suddenly, as Tom's feisty fox terrier appeared from behind the house and started leaping at us in a frenzy.

"It's okay, he's tied," I gasped with relief as a rope pulled him up short. "See, the rope's tied around the porch railing. Let's hope it's not so rotten it pulls loose."

We had scrambled behind the shell of a car, where we were safe, temporarily, from Potato Tom's dog. He was still barking—sharp, warning barks—and jumping up and down on his rope like an organ grinder's monkey.

"Halloo, Patty? What's the trouble?"

It was Potato Tom, standing in the shadow of the doorway, looking every bit as menacing as he had the night we caught him poking in Dugger's trash.

"Someone here?" He stepped out onto the porch.

"Hey, d-does he see us?" Jerry whimpered from his spot at my side.

"I don't think so," I answered uncertainly, all the time keeping my eyes on Potato Tom. Without his long coat, he was patchy, a regular bag of rags, and on his feet he was wearing rubber galoshes.

"Hey, you guys," I whispered, poking them. "The overshoes!"

Potato Tom wheeled around and peered at the car. Then he hobbled, with the help of a cane, to the edge of the porch where he stood staring.

I had not seen him with a cane before.

"S-stay down," Dugger stuttered before I could mention it.

"*Halloo!* Anyone out there?"

We scarcely breathed. Pretty soon, the stillness paid off. Without bothering to check further, Potato Tom scratched his head and shuffled back into the house, although Patty continued barking and pacing to and fro on her leash.

"Let's go," Dugger choked, getting ready to make a break for it.

"Not yet," I insisted. "We've come this far. Let's stay another minute and see if we can spot any of our stuff. Look over there! Some bricks! Jerry, can you tell if they're ours?"

Jerry was in no condition to examine bricks. It was all he could do to creep around to the rear fender of the car and peek at the pile of them a few feet away.

"Well?" Nick hissed.

"I c-can't tell anything," Jerry moaned. "All bricks look alike to me. Come on, you guys, let's move. I'm s-scared."

Big help.

We were all scared.

Crouching low, we made our way around the car to a spot behind the woodpile. "This is a safer place anyhow," Dugger stated, getting back a little of his know-it-allness. "I have a good view of the front porch and can watch the door. You guys check out the rest of the yard. Find out how much of this junk belongs to us."

Several minutes passed and still the dog barked. It seemed odd to me that Potato Tom didn't come out again to investigate, but we saw no one and heard no sound from inside the house.

We heard no sound of him in the house because at that moment he wasn't in the house. He was edging his way around the side of it, where he caught us off guard at the other end of the woodpile and threw us into such a state of panic that we could barely make a move.

"*Run!!*" Nick shouted at the top of his lungs.

"*Run! run!*" Dugger echoed like a stampeded water

buffalo.

We dashed for the woods, stumbling as we ran, our breaths coming out in tearing gasps, our feet pounding across the rock-hard dirt.

"Teke, wait!" I heard a voice call from the vicinity of the shack. Again, louder: "Teke, wait!" and I stopped and turned because I'd know that voice anywhere.

"You guys, hold it! It's my *grandpa!* Look, there, beside Potato Tom. He's calling to us and waving . . . waving for us to come back."

10

"Y OUR grandpa?" Nick asked, disbelieving.

"What's he doing in Potato Tom's shack?" Dugger demanded.

I was at a loss to explain. "How would I know? C'mon, you guys, he's calling us. We'd better go see what he wants."

As we started back toward the house, Jerry said, "Maybe your grandpa's being held prisoner. If he is, this is probably a trick, and we should go call the police."

I shook my head, but the others stopped in their tracks.

"Hey, use some sense! My grandpa wouldn't let us walk into a trap, you know that. We're fellow Buccaneers! He took the blood oath."

They knew this was so, but still, taking that step up onto Potato Tom's porch and following him, and my grandpa, into the rickety old shack was something we'd never planned.

For one thing, it was the first time we'd been close enough to Potato Tom to reach out and touch him. Not that we wanted to, of course. Just standing next to him and looking into those watery old eyes was enough for all of us.

He was not as big a man as I had figured, or as scary.

He was just bone thin and bent over, with a face all crisscrossed with wrinkles. There was almost nothing of him under the pile of clothes he wore. And summer weather or not, he had on heavy pants, a flannel shirt, and a cardigan sweater. It looked like a new sweater, and I was almost certain it was the one my mother had given Grandpa, but I couldn't be sure.

Anyhow, the sweater wasn't important. What was important was that we were there. Buccaneers together in Potato Tom's shack with Grandpa, our newest and very possibly disloyal member, explaining his presence.

"You didn't expect me to spend all my time with you boys, did you?" he asked incredulously. "A man needs some companionship his own age. Old Tom here fits the bill perfectly! He and I get along fine!"

"But Grandpa, you don't understand," I whispered. "Potato Tom's a . . . hermit! We think he's been stealing our supplies."

"I know," Grandpa replied, drawing us aside.

"You *know?*"

"And I've tried to make him stop. But, Tom . . . well, Tom's been collecting junk for so long that he thinks it's all his now. He doesn't distinguish one can of trash from another. He just takes what he needs and goes on to the next pile."

Nick shook his head. "But you didn't tell us! You knew we were worried and you didn't tell us."

"Yeah," Dugger snorted, directing his remarks at me. "What kind of fellow Buccaneer is he? You and all this talk about blood oaths. I knew it wouldn't work. I knew it from the very beginning."

Jerry didn't say anything, but I could tell that he was thinking along the same lines. Oh, maybe not as quick to blame our troubles on a new member as Dugger was— after all, Jerry had been new not too long before, himself —but he was still sorry and disappointed Grandpa had let us down.

And he had let us down. Even I was disillusioned. And yet . . .

"Wait a minute, boys. Teke? Don't go," Grandpa pleaded. "You haven't heard the whole story. Nobody has, since I'm the only one who's even spoken to Tom in over a year. So maybe he did take some things you were saving for the clubhouse . . . he didn't know what he was doing. And he needs your help! Poor Tom's got troubles you've never dreamed of!"

I didn't know what those troubles were but, for Grandpa's sake, I was willing to listen. As for the others, well, Dugger was halfway out the door, but when Jerry hesitated, and then Nick stopped, Dugger came back and stood waiting too.

I slumped down next to Grandpa on the broken-down old sofa.

It was a wonder there was any room on it at all, because the rest of the shack was clutter from top to bottom, worse even than outside, with junk that looked like it'd been moldering there since the Civil War.

Would you believe magazines dating back to the 1930's, stacks of unopened mail, and hundreds of empty soup cans? If Potato Tom had a clean dish left on his shelves to serve soup in, I'd have been surprised. The mug of coffee my grandfather was sipping from took up the only bare spot on the oilcloth-covered table. Smack in the center of it stood Dugger's mother's old statue.

"Boys, to start with, this is my friend Thomas Jackson Wilkins."

First I, and then Jerry, reached out to shake the hand he offered. "That's my name," he said. "Guess I've had people call me Potato Tom for so long that I've near forgot the Christian name my mama gave me."

His hand was frail and trembled some, but I figured this was not unusual for a man who probably ate soup all the time. I asked myself how I could have been so afraid of him before. Up close, he was a pathetic sight. And he looked hurt that Nick and Dugger were ignoring his hand.

I slid my foot to one side and kicked Nick in the ankle.

"Potato . . . I mean, Mr. ah, Wilkins wants to shake hands, Nick!"

Head down, Nick reached out and took Tom's hand. Then he jabbed Dugger in the mid-section with his elbow. "C'mon, Dugger. Shake hands."

Nick's elbow was a convincing factor. "Good to know you," Dugger mumbled, glaring at me all the while. I hoped Grandpa could come up with something convincing. It was going to take a lot of doing to make us all one again.

Grandpa rose to his feet and put his arm around Tom's thin shoulders. "Say what you will, boys, Tom's been fighting to save his place. Those supplies, well, he's been using them to fix things up. Thinks that if he can get his home looking a little better, maybe they won't take it away from him like they're aiming to do."

"What do you mean—take it away from him?" I asked, confused.

"Just that," Grandpa confided. "Those hifalutin dignitaries that run this township are out to get him off this piece of property. Seems they need another park—or say they do—and Tom's land is going to be it. Doesn't matter that he doesn't want to sell, or that there are a host of good places elsewhere. According to them, he belongs in the County Home. They even said they'd make the arrangements so he can get in right away."

Nick sat down on the arm of the sofa, next to me. "But that's not fair. If Mr. Wilkins owns the land he should be able to stay on it for as long as he wants."

Potato Tom sighed. "You'd think so, but I guess that don't matter no more . . . at least not hereabouts."

"You see," Grandpa explained patiently, "a township has the right to condemn land for public use even if it turns out that it never uses it. In many ways, it's a good law, unless it's dragged out to uproot people they just don't want in the community."

I knew for a fact that Potato Tom was not wanted in Primrose Heights. For years, people had been complaining about his place and wanting something done about it. It was a dump, they said, a blight on the community, and yet, it was Potato Tom's home. Even a hermit has a right to be someplace.

"Grandpa? Maybe if—like you said—Mr. Wilkins just cleans things up and paints the house or something, they'll change their minds."

"Possibly," my grandfather replied. "And that's just what he's been trying to do for the past couple months. But it's not easy work, you know, for a man who can't get around well. And this past year has been a bad one for Tom. The fishing hasn't been too good in the creek and what little junk he can collect to sell barely keeps him in spending money."

"I know what you mean about the fishing," I said sympathetically. "Right now, that stream's so polluted a rubber duck couldn't live in it. Those factories up the pike have wrecked it."

Potato Tom nodded. "Nowadays, frogs are the only things I see. Used to catch 'em, too, a while back—real regular—but now they're too fast for me."

He reached down to pet Patty who'd come in and curled at his feet. "Don't seem to register on Patty, though. She still flushes them out, same as ever. Guess she just don't understand."

There was this dead silence as we thought over old Tom's problem and I wondered how I would feel being forced out of my own home. Awful. Worse than awful. But I did not know how the other guys would feel, so I suggested that we go outside for a conference. A secret meeting, actually . . . without Grandpa.

"Well, whatta you want?" Dugger demanded, once we were out on the porch. His arms were folded know-it-all fashion across his chest and I knew just by looking at him that he was going to be a hard guy to convince. Nick and Jerry might be a little easier, even if they weren't all smiles. It was worth a try.

"Jerry? Nick?" I began in hushed tones. "You heard Grandpa say Potato Tom didn't know he was stealing, didn't you? He just took what he needed, and you can't blame him for that, can you? Not when they're trying to take his house."

Nick kicked at a broken floor board. "I . . . I guess not. But your grandpa could have *told* us! I mean, we are . . .

were all members of the same club and all."

I winced when he made us members in the past tense.

"We're still all members of the Buccaneers, as far as I'm concerned," I said. "Jerry? You've always been glad to be part of the club. Don't you think we should stick together now and pitch in to help Tom save his house?"

Jerry looked me straight in the eye, remembering maybe how I'd stuck up for him in the past. "Sure, Teke, I'm willing. C'mon, Nick. The Buccaneers is the best club I've ever been in."

Nick shrugged. "Okay. But I still don't know why your grandpa didn't tell us. I mean, if Old Tom is such a good guy, underneath and all . . . and if he's in trouble . . ."

"Maybe he didn't think we'd be interested," I suggested offhandedly. "My own dad's always saying I'm not interested enough in community problems, and you certainly have to agree Potato Tom's one. Grandpa probably figured the same thing. Maybe thought we just cared about fishing and stuff like that."

Nick nodded, thoughtfully.

Then we turned as one to Dugger, who was still standing on the sidelines, frowning hard. "Dugger, you want to help us haul away junk and paint Tom's shack? We'll need everyone we can get." I paused a moment for effect. "But we'll understand if you say no."

The steely glint disappeared from Dugger's eyes and he looked, disbelieving, at the guys and me. When he could see that we were all together in this thing, it made a difference. After all, he didn't want to be the only one to say no, especially when it meant being left out. So we all shook hands—though somewhat hesitantly—and called another truce.

"So that's our plan," I announced when we stepped back into the shack. "Tomorrow we'll bring some tools and some other stuff and start getting this place looking real neat."

"I . . . I might even be able to bring some paint," Dugger said unexpectedly. "We have a whole cellar full of it, left over from my mother's decorating schemes."

Potato Tom could hardly speak and his watery old eyes got even more watery as he tried to tell us how grateful he was.

"That's okay, sir," I mumbled, finding it a little hard to talk myself. "We just want to help you save your house."

"Yeah," Nick added. "And when we're finished, they won't dare turn you out. The whole town'll be saying what a beautiful place you have."

So we became involved—the four of us—which just shows you how easy it is to get civic-minded at a time when you least expect to.

It was our civic-mindedness that almost got us into trouble the next afternoon when we were hauling away a wagonload of wine bottles. Potato Tom drank a little, so he had boxes full of them, and we had been working for nearly an hour carting them to the nearest trash depot just back of the railroad track.

"Hey, boys, you need some help?" this voice yelled as we struggled to ease the heavy wagon over the tracks.

We looked up. It was Mr. Talbott, our sixth grade teacher, and he was loaded down with a couple of cameras, one of which looked pretty expensive and certainly not the kind of camera he could afford if he is so poor and all, forced to live, as he says, on a teacher's salary.

"Hey, Mr. Talbott," I said, not unfriendly. "What are you doing here?"

"Taking pictures of Primrose Heights' blight," he replied. "For the *Primrose Heights Leader* . . . as a freelance reporter.

"Blight?"

"You know, pollution. Uncollected trash. That sort of thing." He reached down to give us an assist with the wagon. "It's all part of the township's cleanup campaign, though, if you ask me, there are some worse forms of blight in this town than this. Hey, where'd you get all those bottles, anyway? Been hand-picking 'em back in the woods, or did they all come from one place?"

"They're sort of hand-picked," I lied, hoping he'd go away. I figured it would not be too good for him to ask any more questions. He might just decide to trail us back to Potato Tom's, trying to get another picture of some blight.

He didn't ask about following us, but he did want to get a picture.

"Of you boys, you know? How about it, for old times' sake? Four involved members of the younger set, out to do something for their community."

I had sympathy for Mr. Talbott trying to make good on his summer job, but it was not enough. There was this vision in my mind of my mother spotting me in the paper and worrying about where I got all those wine bottles.

"No, Mr. Talbott, it's too risky. I mean, we really don't want the publicity. All we want is to do a good turn; isn't that enough?"

He scratched his head, like he used to do when none of us could catch what he was driving at in class, and said he guessed it was okay. "But, maybe we'll meet again and you won't feel so shy. Call me at home, or at the paper, if you change your minds. I can always use a good story about public-spirited young people. And it'll get me in good with the editor."

As he started to leave, I thought of something he said. "Hey, Mr. Talbott, what did you mean when you said there were even worse forms of blight?"

He shifted his cameras to one side and frowned. "Oh, buying up land that'll never be used. Forcing people into the County Home to do it."

So he'd heard about Potato Tom too. It really didn't

surprise me. In class, Mr. Talbott was always lecturing us on the ills of suburban living, and the world's growing disregard for human rights. He made a lot of sense, but it didn't mean much because what can a teacher do besides talk? It's the big wheels on the boards and the committees of everything who make the decisions. Big wheels like my father—he gets in on a lot of decision making.

Talk about wanting to do something for my community! I was so beat that night when I hit the sheets that the community should have done something for me. My arms and legs felt like they were falling off and I had calluses on my hands from pulling the wagon.

But hauling trash was not the only reason I was miserable. When we arrived home, Grandpa got his letter from Aunt Margaret. It was just as dumb as I thought it would be—filled with all this garbage about how nervous she was and how the doctor advised her to get a full-time job so she wouldn't get bored.

With a full-time job, there'd be no one home to keep Grandpa company. "And so," my mother sniffed, after Grandpa went upstairs to be by himself, "she just said he'd be better off here! Imagine! Oh, Teke, why did he have to write her anyway? I try so hard and still Margaret's his favorite. Margaret—who doesn't give a thought to his feelings half the time!"

11

I WOULDN'T say my grandfather gave up living in the days after that, but he came pretty close to it. Depressed? I had never seen him so down in the dumps. And yet he would not talk about Aunt Margaret's letter to me or anyone else. He just threw himself into the work at Potato Tom's.

It worried me. For one thing, he was trying to do too much.

"Grandpa, come on down. I don't think you should be up on that ladder, at least not in the full sun. It's ninety degrees out, Grandpa. We can let the painting go for a few days. The can says it's better if you apply it when it's less hot and humid anyway."

My grandfather paid no attention. He had a wet handkerchief draped over his head and, for once, had removed his suit coat and was down to his shirt sleeves.

"Teke, do you think your grandpa should be up there?" Jerry asked as he passed me with a wheelbarrow full of garden trash. "I mean, I've noticed he's been breathing kind of hard lately. And he looks a lot more tired . . . you know, even sort of *funny*."

"I've noticed it too, Jerry, but what can I do? He won't listen to anyone and he says he wants to get the house painted before the end of the week."

"There's not much time, you know," Nick added, coming by with a box of petunias. "Your grandpa thinks they'll try to evict Mr. Wilkins any day now."

"Any day?"

"Well, he just found another notice buried in Tom's mail. Don't ask me how long ago it came—the postmark was blurred. It was just there, under all that stuff that's been sitting for weeks."

I remembered Mr. Talbott and wondered if he knew any more about the board's plans than we did. There wouldn't be much hope if the sheriff came to turn Tom out before we were done. His place would have to be shipshape sooner than that. It was the only way the six of us would ever get those officials to change their minds.

I hoped we'd have more luck with the board than I was having with Grandpa. Talk about closed minds, Grandpa's was like a stone wall.

"You gonna quit painting?"

"Nope."

"Well, then, at least come down for a drink of water!"
I shouted, exasperated. I was thinking about what *Every-one's Health* had to say about plenty of fluids. I was also
thinking that my grandfather Kindermann was just about
the stubbornest man I had ever run across.

I waited for a minute, then left the thermos full of cold
water at the foot of the ladder. Nick and Jerry were already
around in front of the house, putting in petunias. Dugger
was on his hands and knees in the garden, helping Potato

Tom plant seeds to replace his vegetable crop.

"I sure hope your mom doesn't notice that some of her plants are missing," I said to Jerry as I jabbed at the ground with a trowel.

"I don't think she will. The rabbits get a lot of them anyway. More'n likely, she'll blame them."

I wished I had the rabbits to blame for the tools I'd "borrowed" from my father's workbench. A paint scraper, some screwdrivers, a hammer, and a half dozen other things —none of which would even interest a rabbit.

It had taken a little doing, but most of the stuff we'd used to fix up Potato Tom's place had come from our own homes. True, some of it would go back, like the extra rakes, shovels, and garden tools, but the petunias, the paint, and a half box of my mother's laundry detergent were there to stay.

I want to tell you, this detergent was just as great as they said on TV. I know, because I personally washed all of Tom's kitchen curtains with it. And when I was done, they were really bright! There were even some little pink flowers in the pattern that I had not noticed before.

Old Tom was so grateful that he invited us to lunch. At first, we'd brought sandwiches from home—explaining to our mothers that we were going to the park, or hiking— but that wouldn't do.

"From now on, you boys eat with me. And call me Tom —not that fancy-sounding Mr. Wilkins. Save that for the big shots. As for me, I ain't so poor that I can't rustle up a little food for my friends. Me and Patty—we'd be honored to have you at our table."

Honored or not, the boys and I were glad for a chance at a real lunch. And the stuff Potato Tom fixed us on that old-fashioned green stove of his was out of this world. For openers, we had soup, bread, beans, and applesauce. After that first lunch Tom put together other combinations; every day we were filled up before we were half through.

Potato Tom I was not so sure of. I mean, maybe he was having trouble with his teeth or his stomach, because every noon he ate the same thing. Half a can of hot soup spooned undiluted over a piece of bread. Sometimes he didn't even bother with the bread. He just heated this thick chunk of soup up in a skillet and ate it straight out of the pan.

I wondered how my grandpa could stand watching him, because Grandpa is always so neat. If he lived to be a million, my grandfather would never eat anything right out of a frying pan. Yet he didn't seem to mind when old Tom did. And I guess I knew why.

Tom Wilkins was gentle and good, the kind of person who got his feelings hurt easily if you, say, wouldn't shake hands with him, or called him a hermit, when what he really was was just an old man, like my grandpa, only different.

We all liked him by that time, even Dugger, which was the biggest surprise of all. I suppose the good eats won him over; it had to be something. Dugger is not keen for old people, especially men, who remind him of his grand-father.

Speaking of grandfathers, mine certainly appreciated Tom's cooking. Yet, one noon, on the day when I had been trying to get him down from the ladder, he didn't stay for lunch.

"Where'd Grandpa go?" I asked, suddenly aware that he was not with us.

"I dunno," Dugger mumbled, his mouth full of bread. "He just said to eat without him. He'll be back later."

Outside, the temperature was up to ninety-two. Wet handkerchief or not, I did not want my grandpa wandering around alone. Maybe I was as bad as my mother, but I didn't care. Grandpa hadn't looked good since he'd received Aunt Margaret's letter. And right then, in all that heat, he was looking worse.

Without touching my lunch, I cut across Tom's land to the railroad tracks. Dugger had seen Grandpa heading toward town. If I hurried, I might catch up with him.

"Grandpa!" I shouted, spotting him a block ahead. "Grandpa, wait!"

He didn't hear. So I kept following, just far enough behind so he would not notice, but just close enough so I could watch where he went.

I found out soon enough. He went straight to Gittleman's Bakery. But this time he didn't buy any doughnuts. Instead he counted something off on his fingers for old Mr. Gittleman, wrote something down in a small notebook, and came out the front door dangling a key in his hand.

From my spot behind the mailbox, I could see pretty well. But I couldn't see where Grandpa went when he climbed the stairs leading to the rooms over Gittleman's store. Nor could I figure out why, if he was such a big doughnut lover, he didn't pick up a dozen of them when he came down ten minutes later.

12

WHATEVER business Grandpa had to talk over with Mr. Gittleman was his own secret, because he did not tell us where he had been when he returned.

I, of course, did not let on that I had been following him. He would have been humiliated. I simply grabbed some leftover beans from the stove, and bolted them down back of the woodpile where he would not notice.

It was a funny thing about my grandpa. He didn't want to be called "old," but he couldn't quite cut it as a kid either. I mean, here he was trying to keep up with the rest of us hauling trash and stuff. It was crazy. Even I knew there was a time to say you were too tired. And for Grandpa that time had come long ago.

So, in the middle of the afternoon, the guys and I decided to try a little strategy of our own.

"Hey! How about if we break for a cold drink?" I suggested, nudging Dugger in the ribs.

"Great idea," he answered with a wink. "What do you say, Mr. Kindermann? It's too hot to work anyway. What was it the last time you looked, Jerry? Ninety-three?"

The four of us had cornered Grandpa on his way to get more paint and if we had to sit on him, he would not get off the porch with another can of it.

"Well," he said as he studied the dripping paint stick in his hands, "I don't know. Still a lot to do, boys. Wouldn't like to see Old Tom wind up in the County Home because I got lazy."

"Oh, Grandpa!" I said with a laugh. "You're not lazy. Besides, the place already looks 100 per cent better than it did when we started. The trash is gone, there are flowers all around, and there's only this one small patch left to paint on the whole house!"

"Teke's right," Nick put in. "Come on, Mr. Kindermann. This little bit can wait till tomorrow. Then *we'll* finish it."

Apparently we convinced Grandpa—at least for the moment. He drank some cold pop with us and then went off to work in a shady corner of the garden. The rest of us hung around near the porch, finishing our sodas and deciding what to start on next.

Suddenly Patty started barking—loud, frenzied "someone's coming" barks, and we all turned around to stare.

"Teke, what is it?"

"I dunno." There was nothing visible near the clearing, just a crunching, rumbling noise coming from an open part of the woods.

Then we saw it!

"You guys!" Nick yelled, before any of us could catch our breath. "Get Tom! We're being invaded!"

I could not believe it. There, crashing toward us, was this gigantic orange bulldozer, its vicious steel blade glinting in the sun.

"Grandpa! Tom! Come quick!"

The heavy-set man tromping alongside the machine had a paper, and as Dugger and Jerry ran to get Potato Tom and my grandfather, he waved it underneath our noses.

"See this? It's an eviction notice! Now where's Thomas Jackson Wilkins?"

I looked around and there was poor old Tom shuffling across the yard between Dugger and Jerry. Grandpa, coming from the garden, had just rounded the corner of the house.

"I'm the sheriff," the big man announced, without even giving Tom a chance to say hello, "and these are your walking papers. Now get what you want to save and move along. There's a crew waiting here. They have work to do."

"Work?" Nick yelled. "You mean you're going to smash Tom's house to bits!"

Potato Tom just stared at the papers and scratched his

head. I figured maybe he couldn't read, he was taking so long to study them, but I was wrong.

He knew the words. He just couldn't believe them.

"I . . . I thought if I fixed up the place, you would leave me alone. The boys said so. Didn't you, boys?"

His eyes puzzled and unhappy, he looked first at me, then at the others for an answer.

It really got to us.

"Who do you think you are?" Dugger blazed at the sheriff. "The Secret Police? Didn't anyone ever tell you it's mean to pick on poor old men?"

"Yeah, mean!" The rest of us echoed, encircling Tom in a protective manner.

The sheriff, who was kind of ruddy-faced anyway, got flaming red. "What are you kids doing here? You some kind of juvenile gang? Get on home, before I call your parents. This is no business of yours."

"Now, just a minute!" My grandpa boomed as he strode forward. "Sheriff or no sheriff, you can't come here like this without warning and threaten this man with a bulldozer! You're still on private property, sir! You come one foot closer to this house with that infernal machine and you'll have to go over my dead body!"

I got the shakes. "Oh, Grandpa. Don't say that!"

The sheriff's eyes got all bulgy. "This is condemned land," he bellowed, shaking his eviction paper at us. "Going to be a public park when we get this dump off it. Now move back, old-timer! Get along, you kids! I don't want to hurt any of you, but I can't guarantee nothing if you're in my way."

Calling my grandfather an old-timer was just about the worst thing he could have done.

"Grandpa? *Grandpa?*" Now I was really scared.

His face and neck were as red as a cooked lobster and his hands were clenched in fury.

"I'm standing pat. Touch this house and you'll have to take me with it!"

"Teke, you've got to do something," Jerry whimpered, tugging at my sleeve. "They'll run him down."

"They wouldn't dare!" I shouted, then in a flash I had an idea. "Tell Grandpa to hold on! I'll try to get help."

Taking a big chance against time, I sprinted for the railroad tracks and the public telephone booth that stood nearby. All the time I was running, I kept thinking about Grandpa and how certain he was to hold the fort right down to the bitter end.

Talk about being scared. I was so chewed up inside I could hardly dial the phone. And then, when the girl at the newspaper office told me to speak slower—she couldn't understand what I was saying—I nearly collapsed.

"Gi-give me Mr. Talbott! Harold Talbott! Please, I've got to t-talk to him. It's an . . . emergency!"

"Hello? Oh, hi there, Teke. Ready to have me take your picture?"

I took a deep breath. "Listen, Mr. Talbott. There's no time to explain, but if you want to help Potato Tom Wilkins, you'd better get over to his place fast!" The sweat from my forehead trickled down my nose. "Quick! Please! They're g-going to smash his house!"

For a second the line seemed dead, then Mr. Talbott's voice snapped over the receiver. "Be right there, Teke. Hang on."

With my heart thumping so hard I could feel it way up in my shoulders, I raced back to the clearing.

"What about my grandpa?" I sputtered when Nick met me halfway. "Is he okay?"

"Just barely," he said tightly and hurried me on.

As we came around the shack I saw what he meant. Grandpa was still holding his ground, but his face had turned a corpselike gray and a vein in his temple throbbed alarmingly.

"Look, mister," the sheriff was saying, in a less demanding voice, "I don't want any trouble. You don't look so good. Why don't you just forget this and let one of my boys take you home?"

Fat chance. Behind him, the mud-splattered bulldozer was growling menacingly, its steel blade poised for action.

"Stop!" I begged, though no one heard me. "Don't you see? We've fixed up Tom's place! You—you haven't even taken time to look."

After gathering up some of his possessions, Old Tom had unchained Patty and was trying to cradle him in his arms, but Patty was having none of it. He wanted to bite the sheriff on the ankle and it was all Nick and Jerry could do to keep him from doing it.

Just then, Dugger grabbed me on the shoulder and spun me around. "Hey, Teke, over there! Isn't that Mr. Talbott? And he's bringing his camera!"

"Camera?" the sheriff roared.

"That's right," Dugger said belligerently. He's a reporter! He takes pictures for the *Primrose Heights Leader!*"

"No pictures!" hollered the sheriff, looking around for his deputy. "Stop that reporter. We've got a job to do here and we can do it without the help of the press."

I did not think our teacher was planning to help him, but there was no time to explain then.

"Hold it, sir. [click]," Mr. Talbott said, snapping a picture of Potato Tom clutching a framed photo and the statue he had rescued from Dugger's trash. The photo was a picture of his mother; who could guess why he wanted the statue?

The sheriff's eyes popped, "Give me that camera!" he growled.

"Not a chance," Mr. Talbott replied, taking pictures right and left. "Hey, who's the old man?" he asked, pointing to my grandfather who was standing stiff and tall on the front porch. "[click] Is he holding 'em off? One more, sir. [click] Terrific!"

Like a real gentleman, Grandpa nodded slightly.

Then, before the sheriff could catch his breath, Mr. Talbott had snapped half a dozen more pictures.

"Out of the way! Deputy, get that thing moving!"

Outraged, the sheriff waved the bulldozer into action, and together, like a clip from some old war movie, they advanced on Mr. Talbott.

"Hey there!" I heard my grandpa gasp in a surprised voice.

"Mr. Talbott," I yelled. "Watch out!"

Talk about agile, Mr. Talbott would have made as good a track star as he was a schoolteacher. First you'd see him jumping around like a rabbit, taking pictures where he could, then he'd be dodging the bulldozer with the camera high above his head.

"Call that thing off," he shouted hoarsely. "You guys losing your minds?"

The man operating the bulldozer hesitated, then looked to the sheriff for instructions.

From the porch, my grandpa taunted, "What's the matter? [cough] The whole lot of you so slow you need a [cough] machine to do your chasing for you?"

The sheriff pretended not to hear. But Grandpa's jab hit home, because the next thing I knew the bulldozer was abandoned and the sheriff's men skirted around the other side of the house where Mr. Talbott had taken refuge.

"Now get him!" the sheriff ordered as Mr. Talbott bolted for his car.

Our sixth grade teacher never had a chance. Even his last-ditch effort to scale the porch railing and get out the

108

other way ended in failure. Two of the sheriff's henchmen tackled him, and the impact threw him flat on his face in the dirt.

Seeing him lying there, still trying to protect his camera from the man straddling him, did something to my senses.

"Come on, you guys," I hollered, ready for a fight. "We gotta help Mr. Talbott!"

But it was a contest that never got off the ground.

Before I'd taken two steps, my grandfather let out a little moan and collapsed in a heap on the back porch.

13

"**D**EAD? No, he's not dead, but he could be, Teke, he could be," Mom said. "Honestly, I don't know if I can ever forgive you for this. To let your grandfather wear himself out that way when a word from you . . . well, just see what's happened!"

My grandpa Kindermann was in the hospital. And I was the sorriest kid in fifty states.

I was more than sorry. I was miserable.

"Mom? I tried to get him to slow down, honest I did, but he just wouldn't listen. The club . . . Potato Tom's . . . he found those on his own. And the guys and I, well, we thought if we kept our eyes on him . . ."

She didn't answer. She just sat at the kitchen table sipping her coffee, waiting with my dad for a phone call from the hospital.

"Ruth, come to bed. You heard what the doctor said . . . Dad's going to be all right. It was a simple case of heat prostration . . . exhaustion, if you want to call it that. In a few days he'll be back home good as new."

My mother stifled a sob. "And all this time I thought he was at the Soaring Sixties. Oh, Walter, I'm sorry I ever pushed the thing so hard. He never liked it. He [sniffle] never liked anything I wanted him to do."

Along with me, she was blaming herself. Because, as she put it, Grandpa never would have been driven to the woods if she'd just let him be.

She was forgetting Mrs. Whitfield's rose garden and all the other crazy things Grandpa did on his own, long before he ever thought of the woods.

"Mom, it's not your fault. He's just that way. Look at the stuff he gets into—he knows it's too much for him, but he just won't admit it. It would be too humiliating. It would be like owning up to the fact that he's old, and you know he doesn't want to do that."

"Teke's right, Ruth. Your dad's just like a kid, and unless an episode like this puts some sense into his head, he's going to keep on acting like one for the rest of his life."

She shook her head. "Never, *never* in my entire life have I met anyone so childish. Yes, you too, Teke. Right now I can't decide which of you is more immature, you or your grandfather!"

I was cut down, but it was only what I deserved.

Me and my secrets. I'd almost killed my grandpa and all because of a few lousy secrets. *Stupid* secrets! Ones that

I never should have been keeping in the first place.

"Mom? I know how mad you are about the club."

"Mmmphh."

"And I'm sorry. First thing tomorrow, I'll turn in my membership."

"I don't think you'll be going anyplace tomorrow," my dad said. "Except for a trip to the hospital, I think you'll be at home for at least a week."

"Yes, sir." It was a small price to pay.

"Sir?" I said later, when my mother had gone to bed. "I suppose you're wishing you never had a son, at least not one as dumb as me."

My father looked up, surprised. "That's ridiculous, T.K. I just wish you'd come to me sooner. Talked things over man to man, before everything got so . . . out of hand."

"I wanted to, sir, but, well, I just couldn't tell you about the club!"

"Why not? I understand about clubs. I even understand about *secret* clubs. Had one myself as a boy."

I tried to picture my father as a boy, but I just couldn't do it. So I said, "Dad? Sometime when . . . ah, all of this is over, will you tell me about your club?"

He gave me a pat on the shoulder. "Sure thing, Teke. I'll even help you build a new clubhouse, someplace closer by where your mother won't worry about you so."

I started upstairs.

"Son? Don't blame yourself entirely for your grandfather's collapse. We're all responsible. I am, your mother is, your grandfather . . . even Aunt Margaret. Ah, yes . . . Margaret. The post office should pay her for every letter she doesn't send."

The next day the doctor said my grandfather was improving, but we were still not over the hump as far as the other complications were concerned.

What's more, the phone had been ringing all day.

Normally, my mom loves talking on the phone. When she doesn't like it is when there's explaining to do. Like how was it that her son and father were involved in a scandal that had them at odds with the sheriff?

"I'm not sure, Sally."

"No, I don't know how long they've been acquainted with that poor old recluse."

"True, it isn't like Teke to . . ."

"Your husband said the township did *what?*"

It wasn't until that night when Mr. Talbott dropped by, his forehead bandaged and his arms scraped and bruised, that my parents were finally clued in on the whole story.

"Talk about public-spirited citizens, Mr. and Mrs. Dearing, your boy Teke is one of the finest! Why, he's practically a hero! All those boys are. Because of them, and that terrific father of yours, old Mr. Wilkins might be able to save his home!"

The news was a surprise to my folks, who'd thought he'd dropped by to discuss my last quarter's grades.

"It's a crime the way they're trying to take Wilkins' home away from him, you know," he said, looking directly at my father. "But now that it's clear of junk, fixed up . . . maybe they'll change their minds."

"That's what we thought," I muttered bitterly. "But they wouldn't even look."

Mr. Talbott smiled at me sympathetically. "I know, Teke, but that's because right now there are only a few of us on Tom's side . . . too few. What we really need is the support of some influential citizens, community leaders, really, to spearhead an action group and put some pressure on the township board."

My father sat straighter. If there is anything he is good at, it is spearheading action groups.

"Walter?" My mother was interested. "Mr. Talbott says the poor soul will have to go to the County Home. Surely you could . . . call someone. Your lodge, maybe? The Jaycees?"

"Dad?" I held my breath.

It was still possible, with all the meetings he was in charge of, that he just didn't have a free night.

He tapped his fingers together and closed his eyes. Then finally he said, "I'll look into it tomorrow, Mr. Talbott, phone a few people. The board'll come around, you'll see. As for me, I'm proud to be of help in this case. Any cause that's good enough to interest my son is good enough for me!"

114

Two days later our club made the newspaper, along with a report that my father's action group had saved Potato Tom's home, and an interview with my grandfather in the hospital.

GOLDEN AGER TAKES COURAGEOUS STAND.

FEELS FIT AS A FIDDLE,

OLDSTER SAYS FROM HOSPITAL BED.

"Hey, Mom, listen to this," I said between spoonfuls of scrambled eggs. "Mr. Kindermann insists the heat and the excitement had nothing whatsoever to do with his collapse. A loose plank was the cause of it. 'Turned my ankle on the fool thing, that's all.'"

"Oh, Walter!"

"Mom?" She was getting back some of her old spunk. "I think maybe we should go along with Grandpa's story about the loose plank. It's embarrassing to him that he's in the hospital!"

"Embarrassing to *him?* Just read some of these newspaper quotes!"

OLDSTER CLAIMS EATING WHAT HE LIKES

AND DOING WHAT HE PLEASES

IS THE SECRET OF HIS PROLONGED YOUTH.

"Well, it hasn't killed him yet," my father murmured, biting into a piece of toast.

"Killed him? Walter, he was taken to the hospital in an *ambulance!* Doesn't that say something about his ridiculous living habits?"

"Now, Ruth, it's like Teke said. He's bullheaded. The harder you push him in the direction you want him to go, the faster he'll run the other way."

My mother sighed. "I suppose you're right. In all the years they were married, my mother never cured him of his stubbornness. I guess I never will, either."

"Right. So will you quit trying and let him enjoy life? He's not going to live forever, you know. Why not let him do what he wants now?"

It was a pretty fair piece of advice, in my opinion, but then my dad never was one for fussing over people. It has always been my mother, and whether or not she could change was up for grabs.

"I don't know, Walter," she said finally. "Let's let the whole thing wait till we pick Dad up at the hospital this noon. Then we can talk it over, arrive at some sensible solution to the whole problem."

Somehow I had the feeling it was too late for that.

And I was right.

When we arrived at the hospital, Grandpa was nowhere around. No one had the slightest idea where he had gone after he'd been discharged.

14

"Y OU ... you let him go on his own? But
I just don't understand. I told Dr. Hollisey we'd be here at
noon."

The nurse's voice was as starchy as her uniform. "Mrs.
Dearing! Your father asked me to call him a cab, said he'd
talked to you on the phone and you couldn't make it."

"Couldn't make it? To pick up my own father?" My
mother was turning colors. "Where's Dr. Hollisey? ... Dr.
Hollisey!"

"Now, Ruth," the doctor said when we finally found him.
"There's no reason why your father shouldn't take a cab
home by himself if he wants. You fuss over him too much.
He's in good health, *remarkable* health for a man his age."

"But, Doctor ..." she interrupted, forgetting all the advice my father'd given her just an hour earlier.

The doctor silenced her with a look. "Of course, I don't
think he should try to . . . ah, keep up with the boys any-

more, but then [chuckle] I doubt if there are many of us who can do that, eh, Walter?"

My father grinned and clapped me on the shoulder. "Right. Teke, why don't you run over to that pay phone and call home. Grandpa's probably there now. We must have just missed him."

I called, but there was no answer.

"Mom? Dad? He's not there. You're not going to like this, but I have this weird feeling that he's run away."

"Run away? Oh, Lord, Walter, what next? Call the police!"

My mother was going to pieces.

"No, wait a minute," I said, stopping them. "I . . . I think I know where he is."

"You *know?*"

"Well, I think I know. But I'm not sure I can convince him to come home. You know how he is . . . and well, now he's twice as unhappy as he ever was because Aunt Margaret doesn't want him back."

"But I want him . . . I always have." My mother was crying.

"I know that, Mom, and I think Grandpa does. But he just doesn't like being told what to do. First, Aunt Margaret tells him he has to come here, then you tell him he has to join the Soaring Sixties, and then *everyone* tells him he can't go back home."

"That's right, Ruth," Dad said. "For the last time, somewhere along the line you have to let him make his own decisions."

"But they're so . . . unpredictable!"

"True, but then, so is your father."

"Mom, shall I see what I can do?"

"Yes, yes, of course, Teke. Tell him I'll change. Promise him . . . anything. *Just get him back home with us where he belongs!*"

What a doll! Not caring who saw, I planted a big kiss right on her cheek and dashed out the hospital door.

It was only three and a half blocks down the street to Gittleman's Bakery. Technically, I was still supposed to be grounded, but it didn't seem to matter then. What mattered was pulling the whole mess out of the fire. Could I do it? A true-blue Buccaneer had to believe he could do anything!

"Mr. Gittleman, do you have rooms to rent over your store? I gotta know, 'cause I'm looking for an old man by the name of Ludwig Theodore Kindermann, and I think I saw him go up there last week."

"Don't know any Ludwig Theodore Kindermann," he snapped back like I was crazy or something. "And who are you anyway, busting in here bothering me with things like that for?"

"Please, Mr. Gittleman. He's my *grandpa*. I'm not here to cause any trouble. I just want to talk to him."

There was no answer.

Then he said, "Your grandpa? Oh, you must be Teke!

Your grandfather told me all about you, son. Says you're a fine boy."

"Can I see him?" I asked, trying not to sound exasperated.

"Well, he said he didn't want any company, but seeing how you're his grandson, I . . . I guess it'll be okay. He's first door to the left at the top of the stairs. Give him my best."

I rushed out of the bakery and pushed open the dirty, splintered door to Gittleman's rooms. The stairs were dark, even in the daytime, and the rubber treads on the steps were old and falling apart.

I do not lie when I say the place smelled. And bad as it was in the entryway, it was even worse upstairs where people lived. I didn't know much about Mr. Gittleman at that time, but I did know he'd gotten a bad decorator. The walls were painted a gloomy olive green and the one window at the top of the stairs was curtainless, with a broken pane.

"Grandpa? Grandpa!" I shouted, pounding on the door marked Number One. "It's me, Teke. Open up!"

For a while there was no sound, then the slow shuffle of feet across the bare floor and the turn of the knob.

"Hello?"

"Grandpa, what are you doing here? We came to pick you up at the hospital. You're supposed to come home."

He just shook his head. "Never. *This* is my home now, boy, my permanent one. Rented it out from Mr. Gittleman last week, but couldn't move in till today because of that fool hospital.

"Look around. I can cook my own meals, come and go as I please, even invite Old Tom over if I like. How'd you find me, anyway?"

"Never mind about that. Grandpa, you can't like it here! It's awful. Look at that sofa . . . it looks like it's been through a couple of fires!"

He did not like me criticizing his sofa. "It's comfortable enough," he said, bristling. "Just because something's a little . . . plain doesn't mean it's no good!"

I could see I was getting nowhere with my forthright approach. Grandpa was still Grandpa, and he would never admit he was making a mistake if he lived to be a million years old.

So I got smart. "You know, maybe you're right . . . about this place, I mean. You've got your own room, the bakery's right downstairs, and there's no one around to bother you. Not me . . . not anyone!"

My grandfather looked surprised. "Oh, it wasn't you, Teke . . ."

"I know, it was my mother. What a fusser. Always worrying, babying people half to death. Too bad she can't be more like Aunt Margaret. Aunt Margaret doesn't care what a person does."

Grandpa shuffled over to the window and looked out at the traffic. "Margaret has her faults."

"Yeah, but not many, I bet. Boy, I can sure see that she's your favorite," I rattled on heartlessly. "Never fussing. Never *bothering* you in any way. When Mom loves someone, she's a regular worrywart."

"Your mother's a lot like your grandma."

"Uh-huh."

"Fine woman, your grandma. Even if she was a bit bossy."

I turned to go. "Well, I'll tell Mom and Dad to send over your things. You want them tonight, or will any old day be just as good?"

"Any . . . old . . . day, I guess," he answered sadly. "Teke?"

"Yes, Grandpa?"

"I could come by for them myself, you know. Maybe even visit for a while. Let your mom know I'm all right."

"Well, *I'll* tell her. 'Course, she'd like to see for herself, I suppose. You know Mom."

"Maybe . . . maybe I'll drop by tonight, then. Just for a couple of minutes."

"Great," I said. "And Grandpa? If you ever get tired of this place, decide it's too small or something, we'd like to have you back."

"You would?"

"We all would."

He was silent for a few minutes, then he sat down on the edge of his bed and surveyed the room. "It *is* small. Kind

of stuffy, even. You notice that smell, boy?"

It had gotten to him too. "It's not *real* bad, Grandpa. You can open the windows, can't you? Or do you get too many exhaust fumes from off the street?"

He got too many exhaust fumes from off the street.

"Teke? Maybe I was too hasty picking a place on the second floor. The stairs, you know. I really shouldn't be climbing all those stairs."

I said nothing.

"I could tell Mr. Gittleman I've changed my mind," he suggested timidly. "Maybe go home with you and wait around till I find something better in the want ads."

"If you *want* to, Grandpa. I'm sure Mom won't bother you. None of us will. From now on, you can do just as you please."

"I can?"

"Sure. There's just one thing, though. A few things."

"What's that?"

"If you come back, I really think you should stop bragging up Aunt Margaret all the time. It hurts my mother's feelings."

"And . . . ?"

"You could stop calling my father Walton. His name's *Wal-ter*."

Grandpa got this sly smile on his face like he knew it all the time. "Wal-ter. Now, is there anything else?"

"Stop running down Grandma. Say something nice about

her once in a while. And take an afternoon off to shop for some new shoes. After all your hiking through the woods, these are . . . ah, about worn out."

"Okay, you drive a hard bargain. But, Teke, I'll tell you this right now. Starting tomorrow, I won't have time for your Buccaneers. I have my own friends now—by that I mean friends my own age, like Sam Gittleman and Tom— and I need time with them. You understand, boy, don't you?"

"Sure, Grandpa," I said, more disappointed than I'd figured on being.

He gave me the X-ray eye.

"That doesn't change anything as far as you and I are concerned, though, Teke. We're *best* friends. And nothing's better than that, right?"

"Right, Grandpa." I was awfully glad he was mine. Grandpas like him don't come along very often.

You may wonder what happened then. Like did I ever get another clubhouse and did Grandpa come back to live with us permanently? The answer to both questions is yes, although as far as living with us is concerned, Grandpa won't admit it's permanent. He is with us "temporarily" or just until he can find himself a decent apartment.

I do not argue with this. Checking the want ads every night (even if he never finds anything) gives Grandpa the feeling that he is on top of things. It also keeps my mother on her toes, which is okay because she still has this tendency to fuss even now after all the trouble we went through getting Grandpa and saving Potato Tom.

Speaking of Potato Tom, he is almost a celebrity. Suddenly a lot of folks who never thought about him before are bringing him food baskets, grass seed, and hand-me-down clothes. I guess they figure he is there for good, and they might as well make the best of it.

What Old Tom thinks about this I do not know. I just know that sometimes, when he gets a particularly choice basket of food, he calls my Grandpa and the two of them batch it for the weekend at Tom's shack.

This is okay with me. I have my own things to do. Like scrounging for old wood to camouflage the clubhouse that my father built for us out of new lumber.

Dad's forgotten that clubhouses look best when they are old and beat up. But he is still a fair handyman. He fixed things up so Grandpa and I would not have to share a room anymore, by partitioning off my old bedroom into two rooms. The only trouble is the wall is not soundproof and some nights I still hear that familiar "aaghnn-nn" as I drift off to sleep.

No matter. I'm getting used to it. You can get used to a lot of things if you really want to.